LOVE BY THE BOOKS

TÉ RUSS

CONTENTS

To Miss CCJ: Thanks for the encouragement to "Dooo it!" ;-)

Hello all!

Writing this book was a brand-new endeavor for me. It took me to a place I hadn't been in nearly a decade: writing a story in the first person point of view. I'll admit, when the thought to do it first came to me, it felt quite daunting and I was intimidated. But I'm thankful for the support system I have and everyone who encouraged me through this process.

And if you're wondering, "Why now?" the simple answer is this is how the characters demanded I write the story.

I couldn't have written Carmen and Sebastian's story any other way. This was truly a labor of love, and I hope you enjoy reading it, as much as I enjoyed writing it!

Happy Reading,

Té

CHAPTER ONE

Carmen

"**Y**ou *can't* be serious!"

I stopped walking, pulled my phone away from my face and glared at it, as if the man on the other end of the line could see the expression on my face. Letting out an exasperated sigh, I put the phone back up to my ear and said, "You know damn well, that I'm completely serious."

I started walking again, weaving my way through the crowded sidewalk and the man on the phone said, "Carmen, the amount you're asking – for a debut author, it's unheard of!"

"And the profits you'll make from this debut author within the first *week* will be unheard of," I said. "And I haven't even mentioned movie rights yet."

"You actually think the book is *that* good?"

"I *know* it's that good. I wouldn't be pitching it to you if it wasn't that good. And I know you're looking for something to redeem yourself after that last flop of a book turned movie."

I stopped walking again, holding my breath, because

well...I'd just played my trump card, my ace in the whole, my Hail Mary.

You get the picture.

"Carmen," he sighed.

"Look," I said, feigning indifference. "You either sign him with the advance we're asking for or I'll shop him with another publishing company. That's all there is to it."

But that *wasn't* all there was to it.

This moment was all there was to it, because this was our last hope. Every other publishing company had turned my client and his book down. His amazing, definite best-seller in the making book.

Bobby needed this win.

I needed this win.

Another sigh came through the phone and then, "You *sure* he's worth it?"

"He has a great book. I guarantee that there will be a bidding war between the production companies over the movie rights and it's *going* to be a great movie in the hands of the right studio. In fact, it could be the next blockbuster franchise of movies. Bobby is already working on book *three*. And he's easy on the eyes. Women will eat him up. It's like you're getting the trifecta. Now the question is, do you want *your* publishing company to be the one raking in all the money from his success? Or will you be sitting up there in your office regretting that you didn't listen to me?"

I could hear the faint tapping of a pen on the desk through the phone. My grip tightened nervously around my purse strap and then I heard one final sigh.

The sigh of concession.

"Fine, Carmen. You've got a deal."

I nearly yelped and jumped in the air with excitement.

But my hip hugging, knee-length pencil skirt and four inch stilettos didn't allow for such celebrations.

So instead, I calmly said, "I would like the contract in my inbox in the next fifteen minutes for Bobby to sign."

Once he agreed, I said goodbye and hung up the phone.

I turned and looked up at the sign in the window where Bobby wanted me to meet him. The place where he'd apparently spent much of his time creating the books that I'd just gotten him a multimillion-dollar advance on.

How I, Carmen Jones, lover of all things books, had never stumbled across this quaint little bookstore – By the Books – was beyond me.

The moment I walked in, I felt right at home. As I did every time I walked into an old bookstore, I took a deep breath and my nerves calmed instantly.

One intriguing thing about this bookstore was the long bar against the wall.

The man behind the bar was *more* intriguing. He was leaning against a tall pillar, one leg clearly propped up on a shelf. He was gorgeous – with his honey-kissed skin, low cut waves on his head I could imagine swimming my fingers through, and strong jawline that was slightly tense as his dark eyes narrowed in thought. My eyes traveled down to his strong arms, and then down to his hands, which held the book he was clearly absorbed in reading.

It was the sexiest thing I'd seen, probably ever. The sapiosexual in me was having a field day with watching the man so engrossed in his book. One of his long fingers reached up to the top of the book and gingerly turned the page and I literally had to bite back a moan.

It had been *way* too long since I'd had sex.

But being a literary agent – being the *best* damn literary agent – didn't leave much time for a social life.

So here I was, standing in the middle of a bookstore, about to have a damn orgasm from merely watching a sexy ass man reading a book.

As if sensing my odd voyeuristic self, he looked up. Right into my eyes.

I stood there frozen as he watched me, watching him. His lip curled up slightly, revealing a dimple. No man who was this fine had any business having a dimple. My panties might as well have just singed off.

"Carmen!"

I blinked and finally turned my gaze away from what I knew would be the object of my wet dreams for many nights to come and smiled at Bobby, who was hurrying toward me as he came down one of the aisles of books. He had a hopeful look in his eyes. The same hopeful look he had in his eyes when I'd called him to my office after I'd spent all night reading the book he'd submitted and I *knew* I was holding a future bestseller. The same hopeful look that he had when I offered to be his literary agent. The same hopeful look that I saw diminish over time when we received rejection after rejection by nearly every publishing company because they couldn't see what I saw.

I hated seeing that hope fade.

"Well," he said, when he stood in front of me, wringing his hands.

My phone pinged and I held up a finger to Bobby and looked at my phone.

It was the email.

I unlocked my phone, opened the email and said, "Bobby Archer, how does it feel to be a multimillionaire?"

Bobby's eyes nearly popped out of his sockets.

"What?" he rasped.

I quickly scrolled through the email until I reached the

compensation portion of the contract and then turned my phone around so Bobby could see the figure.

"That's – *that's* what I'm getting?" he asked, looking as if he might faint.

I nodded, my lips spreading into a wide grin.

"You did it, Bobby!" I said proudly.

Bobby shook his head slowly and then he let out the loudest whoop, causing everyone to turn to look in our direction. He kept whooping over and over, and then he picked me up and spun me around in a full circle, before setting me back on my feet and hugging me tightly.

"*You* did it, Carmen," he said, when he released me and I noticed his eyes were actually glistening. "You were one of the few people who believed in me, and believed in my stories. And now–"

"You're gonna be a famous writer," I said.

"I'm gonna be a famous writer!" he shouted and the patrons in the bookstore seemed to feed off of Bobby's energy as they clapped and cheered for him. Bobby turned to the sexy reader and said, "Bas, drinks for everyone! On me."

We made our way over to the bar where Mr. Sexy Reader – a/k/a Bas, as Bobby had fondly referred to him – was still watching us. He grabbed a napkin and tucked it between the pages of his book as a bookmark and put it under the bar. It was good to know he wasn't one of those page-folding monsters.

He deftly lined the bar with several shot glasses, and then turned to grab a bottle from the shelf from behind him. I was slightly surprised to see it was tequila. I took a better look at the shelf and realized that it was stocked with quite a few different spirits.

As he quickly filled each glass, Bobby said, "Bas, this is

the agent I was telling you about. *My* agent." He shook his head in disbelief, as he added, "I have an agent."

"Yes, you do," I said.

Bobby got back to the introductions, which I was incredibly eager for.

"Carmen Jones, this is Sebastian Kincaid."

Sebastian sat the bottle down, wiped his hand on the towel that was slung over his shoulder, and held it out to me.

"Pleasure to meet you," he said, setting off a host of butterflies in my stomach.

I reached over and accepted his outstretched hand and those damn flutters in my stomach only intensified.

"Likewise," I said.

He gave my hand a gentle squeeze before releasing it and went back to pouring shots.

"So," he said, looking at Bobby with a teasing glint in his eyes, "You're not going to be too good to write here in our humble establishment now that you're 'Robert Archer', the rich and famous crime thriller novelist, are you?"

Bobby, who'd been passing out shots to the people behind him, stopped and shook his head.

"No way, man," he insisted. "This place is like home."

Sebastian nodded and picked up the last shot glass.

"To Bobby!" he shouted and everyone echoed the accolade, myself included.

We all clinked our glasses together, and my eyes locked with Sebastian's as we toasted.

He gave me a sinful grin before tossing a shot back with the rest of us and then came from around the bar and pulled Bobby into a tight, brotherly hug.

"Seriously though, congrats. I know you've worked your ass off to get this."

"Thanks man," Bobby said.

I watched Sebastian make his way back behind the bar. The back of him looking just as delicious as the front in his well-worn jeans, and found myself asking, "Your boss won't mind you drinking on the job?"

He looked me in the eyes and his mouth spread into a smile, showing off his white teeth.

"Nah," Sebastian said. "He won't trip off one shot."

"He must be a great boss."

"Actually, he's quite a hard ass."

Before I got to say anything else, Bobby walked back to the bar with his wife, Ellie, who'd just arrived.

"Is it true?" she asked. "Did he really get a deal?"

I nodded, and her eyes filled with tears before she pulled me into a hug and sobbed on my shoulder. I let her get her cry out. They'd been having a rough time lately. They'd fallen behind on their mortgage, and their third baby was on the way. But even with all their hardships, Ellie still supported Bobby and his dream to one day have his work published.

"Thank you," she said, when she finally pulled away. "You know how I've worried about him working at that dangerous factory job."

I squeezed Ellie's shoulders as I said, "That's not something you'll have to worry about anymore."

"We're going to dinner to celebrate," Bobby said. "We want you to join us."

"Oh." I looked over my shoulder. Everyone had gone back to what they were doing before Bobby received the great news, including Sebastian. He had his book open in his hands again, turning to the page he'd bookmarked.

I didn't want to leave. Part of the reason was because I hadn't gotten the chance to explore the large two-story establishment, which seemed to be a bookstore/coffee house/bar. The other reason had chosen that moment to look up to catch me staring at him again. I could honestly just sit and watch him read all day – not like *that* was creepy or anything.

I quickly turned and smiled at Bobby and Ellie.

"I'd love to," I said. "But dinner is on me."

Bobby opened his mouth to argue, but I held up my hand to stop him. "I insist."

Bobby hesitated for a moment and then nodded. "Let me settle my tab and I'll meet the two of you outside."

When I got to the door and held it open for Ellie, I noticed Sebastian pushing Bobby's hand away, which was holding his credit card, and shook his head. Bobby asked Sebastian something and Sebastian nodded and waved Bobby off. Bobby made his way to the door, shoving his credit card back in his wallet, and I locked eyes with Sebastian one last time.

His lip tilted up, and those butterflies came back when he called out to me and said, "Don't be a stranger, Carmen Jones."

CHAPTER TWO

Carmen

Dinner with Bobby and Ella had been great. But I was so grateful when I got on the elevator that would take me home to my condominium. As the elevator crawled its way to the tenth floor, I kicked off my heels and bent down to pick them up. With my shoes in one hand and a bottle of champagne in the other hand, I exited the elevator when the automated voice announced that it had arrived at my destination. I trudged down the hall, smiling as I heard my neighbor, Donatello, the opera singer.

Some of the other neighbors found his singing to be a disturbance. I found it to be comforting. I stopped for a moment, wanting to knock on his door to tell him the good news of closing the book deal for Bobby, but decided I'd tell him later and let him finish his practice. He had a show coming soon, which I had two free tickets to attend.

I continued to my apartment, sitting my shoes down for a moment to dig my keys out of my purse. I unlocked the door, grabbed my shoes and went inside. I fell back against the door and let out a content breath as I looked around.

Thanks to the deal, my commission from it would get me back on top of my finances, which were in dire straits.

My eyes fell to the closet door that housed a box that I hadn't touched in over a year. The box that I'd carried home the day I was fired from my job at one of the top literary agencies in the country. My temper flared at the memory of the day my boss sat me down to let me know that I was being terminated.

I'd gone into his office expecting – *deserving* – a raise. But instead, he'd decided to go the route of nepotism, choosing to give his nephew a pay increase, while stabbing me in the back.

Oh, the hell I raised that day. I stormed out of my office, with my head held high, fire in my eyes and determination in my blood, reminding them of the millions and millions of dollars I'd made them, vowing to the entire room that they'd 'rue the day' that they let me go.

Yes, I *literally* said 'rue the day'. I was highly dramatic. And it was quite the Jerry Maguire moment. Unfortunately, so was the aftermath, when client after client let me know that they were sticking with the agency.

The only thing that had kept me afloat over the last year was my savings; however, that had begun to dwindle several months ago.

But now, thanks to a hefty fifteen percent commission that would be hitting my bank account soon, I'd no longer have to survive off peanut butter and jelly sandwiches and noodles. I could also get my mortgage out of default status. Bobby and Ella hadn't been the only ones struggling when he reached out to me to be his agent.

I pushed myself off the door and walked toward the kitchen, tossing my shoes to the floor. I pulled out the wine opener and grabbed a glass from the mounted rack. Once I opened the bottle, I filled my glass to the top and then walked through the condo to my bedroom.

For the last month, I'd had a recurring dream that I'd have to downsize to one of those tiny homes that seemed to be all the rage now. The thought of having to sell this place made me shiver. Yes, a three bedroom, three bathrooms, two thousand square foot condo may have seemed excessive for a single woman, who didn't appear to have a single romantic prospect, but I liked my space.

And dammit, I'd worked my ass off to get this place.

But as I finished my glass of wine, I stripped out of my clothes before sliding into bed. I had a feeling that there'd be no tiny home nightmares tonight.

I woke up late the next morning, after the best sleep I'd had in months. I got out of bed, grabbed some fresh clothes and took a long hot shower. I even appreciated the hot water a little more, knowing I wouldn't be losing it.

I washed, conditioned and detangled my hair in the shower, while I sang along to the streaming radio app on my tablet blasting through the built-in speakers.

I finally got out, lathered myself in body butter after I dried off and got dressed. I went to the kitchen, where I'd left my purse the night before and searched around in it for my phone. When I discovered it was dead, I plugged it in to charge, while I started preparing breakfast.

My coffee machine had just finished filling up my over-sized mug when I heard the buzz alerting that it was on. As I stirred the cream and sugar in my coffee, I turned when my phone let out a slew of pings. My brow furrowed wondering who in the world could be blowing up my phone.

I went to pick it up, my eyes grew wide when I looked at the ten missed calls and voicemails, and a few text messages. Before I could begin to check them, my phone rang.

I smiled when I saw that it was Heather Braggs, one of my best friends and my former secretary. When I'd made my grand exit from the agency, a part of me had hoped Heather would ride out with me. But Heather wasn't the 'ride or die' type. She had questions, like "Are we going to have health insurance? My kid is going to need braces."

They were perfectly logical questions and I held no grudge towards her for wanting to continue making a steady income. She came over the night I was fired and cried with me while we drowned ourselves in liquor and ice cream.

"Hey," I said as I answered the phone.

"Congratulations!" she shouted.

"How'd you find out?" I asked, confused. I hadn't told her, or anyone, about the book deal yet.

"You're kidding, right?" Heather asked. "Honey, go to Publish Now's website."

I hurried to my office, coffee in hand, and opened my laptop. When I pulled up the site, I nearly dropped my mug at the sight of the main headline.

Debut Author Inks Unprecedented Book Deal

"Oh my!"

"Crime thriller author, Robert Archer, inks a book deal with one of the top publishing agents..." Heather was reading the article and I followed along on my computer. "The deal, brokered by Carmen Jones, former agent with

Mason and Dunn Literary Agency, is said to be one of the biggest payouts in literary history!"

Heather's voice grew higher and higher with each word she read until she began to squeal with delight.

"Aren't you at work?" I asked Heather, worried she was going to cause a scene.

"I took a 'smoke break'," she said. Heather didn't smoke, but she took advantage of the perk. She lowered her voice as she said, "Honey, they are losing their shit around here over this."

With Heather still working there, she was kind of like an informant of sorts. And it put a huge smile of satisfaction on my face to know that they were sick because of this deal I'd made by myself.

"This is it, you know?" Heather said, excitedly. "The one deal you needed to turn everything around."

I felt it too. I felt the shift in the atmosphere, like my life was about to take a turn for the better.

We chatted for a few more minutes and then I hung up. I finally began to check my voicemails.

To my surprise, half of them were from some of my former clients. The other half were from authors who were clients of other agents at my old agency. Apparently, they'd also heard of the book deal I'd scored for Bobby and they were suddenly eager to talk.

And I was more than ready to listen.

I spun around in my chair, giddy with excitement as I shouted, "I'm back!"

CHAPTER THREE

Sebastian

E very time that damn door opened, I found myself looking up hoping to see her walk in. It had been a week since she'd come in giving Bobby the life changing news that she'd gotten him a book deal.

I'd seen Bobby since then. He'd come in to show me how he'd made the top headline on the home page of Publish Now's website.

But no Carmen.

"Why don't you just ask Bobby about her, instead of looking like a sad puppy every time the door opens?"

I rolled my eyes before turning to Suzette, my younger cousin and my barista/bartender. She was the reason that I'd been working behind the bar all day. She'd had a full day of classes and couldn't come into work until later in the afternoon, so I'd stepped in for her.

It had been so worth it, when I looked up to find the gorgeous woman, with toasted almond colored skin and striking grey eyes, staring curiously at me.

I still remembered the way her blouse hugged her

breasts, the way her skirt showed off her round sexy ass, and her heels seemed to accentuate her long legs that I envisioned wrapped around me as I dove in and out of her–

The bell over the door rang, jerking me out of my fantasy. A couple of college students walked in and I heard Suzette chuckle behind me as she added whipped cream to a latte. Rather than hear her continue to get on my case, I decided to start restocking the shelves with our latest shipment of books.

I grabbed a box from the storage room in the back, cut it open and then carried it up to the second floor. I sat the box down on one of the carts we kept up there for this specific reason and began to make my way through the aisles, refilling the shelves with books we'd sold out on.

I rounded the corner of one of the aisles and stopped. Sitting at one of the tables hidden away in the back, was Carmen, lost in a book. Those sexy ass lips of hers were wrapped around a straw sipping out of one of our signature cups.

She looked *completely* different from when we'd met a week ago. Gone were the business clothes and neat bun. Now her hair fell past her shoulders in wild, corkscrew curls that had my fingers suddenly itching with a desire to run through them. She was wearing an unbuttoned plaid shirt with a white tank top underneath, jeans and some kind of wedge heel. A pair of cat eye glasses were perched on the tip of her cute nose, and she kept pushing them up on her face.

She was the sexiest black nerd I'd ever seen.

I couldn't gauge how long she'd been sitting there, but she looked comfortable and even though I'd been hoping to see her again – more than I cared to admit – I didn't want to disturb her. But just as I was about to push the cart full of books down another aisle, Carmen looked up.

Her face broke into a huge smile when she saw me, and I found myself smiling back at her.

"Sebastian!"

The sound of my name on her lips stirred something in me. It had me wondering what it would sound like as she moaned breathlessly from my relentless strokes.

"Looks like you're really into that book," I said, abandoning the cart to make my way over to where she was sitting.

Her cheeks heated as she closed the book and pushed it to the side, but not before I got a glimpse of the cover.

"Noble Surrender," I murmured, before looking back at her. "Must have been getting good."

"It was," she said.

"If I'm interrupting, I can get back to wor–"

"No!" she said quickly, sitting up a bit straighter. She pulled her bottom lip between her teeth. "I mean...if *you're* not too busy."

"Nah," I said, as I pulled out the chair across from her and sat down. We sat there staring at each other for an awkward moment before I finally spoke. "What were you reading that had you so engrossed?"

She waved her hand, the blush in her cheeks deepening even more. "There was a scene with an aerial hammock...and...other things going on. You know, you should just read it. I wouldn't want to spoil it for you."

I shook my head. "Romance isn't really a preferred reading genre of mine."

Carmen laughed and the sound seemed to dance across my skin.

"Oh, come on, you should give it a shot. You never know, you might actually like it."

"I'll pass," I chuckled.

"Plenty of men read romance novels you know," she pointed out.

"Maybe so, but I don't see myself being one of those guys."

She shrugged, took a sip of her drink and then asked, "So what were *you* reading the other day when I came by with the good news for Bobby?"

"Before the Fall," I said.

Carmen gasped, "That was a *great* book!"

"You've read it?"

"Of course, I have," Carmen said. "And if you enjoyed that, you'll *love* Bobby's book."

"I did love it," I said, sitting back.

"You've read it already?" she asked.

"I sure have. I was the one who suggested he submit his manuscript."

"Well then, I guess I have you to thank," she murmured.

"What was that?"

"Oh," she shook her head. "It's nothing really. I've kind of been trying to give the whole literary agent thing a go on my own. I was let go from my job last year."

"I'm sorry to hear that," I said.

Carmen waved off the apology as she continued, "I reached out to a friend over at Publish Now and had an ad placed on their site seeking new clients and..."

"And Bobby submitted his work to you," I finished.

Carmen nodded.

"I couldn't put it down," she whispered, leaning forward. "I mean, have you *ever* read anything quite like that?"

"No, actually, I can't say that I have. I can definitely see those books on the big screen one day."

Her lip tilted up in a conspiratorial grin as she said, "If I have my way, that's definitely going to happen."

"So, you're a cold ass literary agent, huh?"

"Well, I don't mean to brag," she teased, shrugging again.

"Nah, if you're good at what you do, by all means, brag."

Her smile dimmed slightly as she said, "It's been a rough year, but I think things are starting to look up now."

"That's good," I said and reached over to pat her hand encouragingly.

Her phone pinged at that moment and she pulled her hand from under mine to reach for her phone.

"Shit," she said, hopping up. "I lost track of time. I'm meeting a friend for lunch."

She quickly picked up her bag and I stood as well.

"I want to see you again," I blurted out. She was in a hurry, so there was no use in beating around the bush.

She slowed down at my words and smiled.

"When?" she asked.

"Do you have a pen?" I asked as I pulled one of my business cards out of my wallet.

She dug into her bag and found one. After she handed it to me, I scribbled on the back of my card, as I said, "Meet me here on Saturday night."

I gave her the card and the pen back and she looked at the card, her brows scrunching up in confusion.

"Hemingway? What is this? Saturday's Wi-Fi password or something?"

I chuckled. "Not exactly. Just say that to the barista when you get here." I let my eyes boldly rake over her body, before adding, "Dress code is cocktail attire."

She tapped the card on her chin for a moment before nodding. "Okay, Saturday. What time should I get here?"

"Is eight good for you?"

"Works for me." Her phone pinged again. "Damn, I've really have to go or my friend is going to kill me."

But even though she had somewhere to be, she didn't seem to be in a rush as she slowly backed away, keeping her eyes on mine.

She lost her balance on her shoes and I took a step toward her.

"Are you okay?" I asked, slightly alarmed.

She held up her hand as she let out a cute little laugh/snort at herself, and then clasped her hand over her mouth.

"I'm fine," she finally said after she removed her hand and rolled her eyes, appearing flustered as she ran her fingers through her hair.

"I'll see you Saturday," I said, unable to fight a grin.

"See you Saturday," she replied, before turning and disappearing down an aisle toward the stairs.

I turned, preparing to get back to work, when my eyes landed on the newly vacated table and the book Carmen seemed to have forgotten all about.

I reached over, snatched it up and hurried down the stairs. I rushed through the first floor of the bookstore and out the front door, but she was nowhere in sight. I turned, went back inside, ducking between the aisles so I wouldn't have to hear Suzette and her big mouth, and headed for the stairs.

When I made it back upstairs, I absently flipped through the pages of the book, landing on the page Carmen had bookmarked. I leisurely skimmed over the words and my eyes grew wide as I read about the aerial hammock

Carmen had mentioned earlier, and the things Ian was doing to Giselle in said hammock.

"Damn," I whispered as I sank down in a chair at a table.

Maybe I *should* give these books a try.

CHAPTER FOUR

I rushed into the restaurant and scanned the place until I found Heather.

"I'm so sorry," I said as I slid into the booth across from her.

"Girl, please, I just got here myself," Heather replied flippantly. She smiled and reached across the table and took my hand in hers as she said, "You look good, girl. I've missed you."

"I've missed you too," I said, blinking away tears. "I'm sorry that I've been acting like a hermit lately."

Heather swiped away a tear of her own as she said, "I thought maybe you were still mad at me for not leaving the agency when you did."

"What?" I asked, shocked. I shook my head quickly as I said, "Honey, you know I'd never ask you to do something like that. You have to make a living, and you have Tevin to think about."

Tevin was Heather's ten-year-old son.

"After I got fired, I shut myself off from the rest of the

world while I tried to climb my way back up to the top. But I realize that I shouldn't have done that," I said regretfully.

"No, you shouldn't have," Heather said. "But you're here now."

It felt good too. I'd gone from seeing Heather every day, to occasional lunches when I wasn't too busy wallowing in my own self-pity. It was unhealthy. But I finally pulled up my big girl panties and got back to work, hunting for clients. I'd told Mason and Dunn Literary Agency that they'd regret letting me go and sitting around pouting all day wasn't going to get the job done.

I hadn't earned the nickname 'Cut-Throat Carmen' by just hoping for the best. I got out there and made shit happen. The literary world needed a stark reminder of who the hell I was, and getting that deal for Bobby had done it.

"So," Heather said, after the waiter had taken our drink orders. "Word around the water cooler at the agency is that a certain former agent is snatching back some of her old clients and adding some new ones to her roster as well."

"Is that what you heard?" I asked, my voice full of mock innocence.

Heather grinned and shook her head. "You know I'm crazy proud of you, right?"

"Proud enough to join me, if I were to offer you a job?"

"What?" Heather asked. "Are you serious, Carmen?"

The waiter returned before I could answer, setting our drinks down on the table. We quickly gave him our orders and once he was gone, I looked up to find Heather staring at me expectantly.

"Okay," I started. "Of course, when I got fired from Mason and Dunn, there was *no* way I could afford you. Not with those bastards undercutting me of all my clients. But from the commission from Bobby's book deal alone, it may take a couple of months to get everything in place, but I'd like to make you an offer."

"What kind of offer?" she leaned forward and asked curiously.

"Twenty percent more than what you're making now, plus full benefits."

"I'm in."

My eyes grew wide. "But...you didn't even take the time to think about it."

Heather smiled as she said, "Carmen, I always knew this day would come. I knew you were going to branch out on your own. And let's face it, you kinda need me."

She said the last part teasingly, but it was *so* true. Heather was the best at keeping me organized and sane. Which, in turn, allowed me to keep my clients organized and sane.

We'd been a team before and if I was going to do this on my own, it wouldn't work without Heather.

"So, when can I put in my notice?" she asked.

"Like I said, it might take a couple of months. I still have to get my commission check from Bobby's advance."

Heather nodded. "Anything you need in the meantime, just let me know."

"I couldn't ask you to–"

"*You* aren't asking me. I'm telling you. I've got your back, so let me be there for you."

"Okay," I said, nodding. "I can't believe all of this happened in the blink of an eye. It's like something you'd read in a book or see on a movie."

"It *didn't* happen in the blink of an eye," Heather said. The waiter brought our food and she pointed at me with her fork as she added, "You've been busting your ass searching for clients and when you finally got one, like you *always* do, you got out there and pounded the pavement to get Bobby that book deal. And it finally paid off. Your old clients were reminded of just how hard you're willing to work for them and the potentially new ones saw the same thing."

Heather had always had a way of putting things into a better perspective.

We dug into our food and the moments of quiet gave my mind the opportunity to drift off to Sebastian and our...date? Was it a date? He'd asked me to meet him at the bookstore, but he said to dress in cocktail attire. It seemed a little too formal just to be hanging out having coffee, even if it was spiked.

I decided that since the restaurant I was meeting Heather at was on the way, I'd drop by the bookstore for a little while and really explore the place, since I hadn't gotten the chance to when I was there to meet Bobby.

It was even better than my initial observation had led me to believe. I'd grabbed an iced coffee from the bar, where I learned that after five, you could add a splash or more of something a bit stronger to the drinks. They had an entire menu of spiked coffees. I looked forward to making an evening trip.

I browsed the first floor of the store for a while, and then made my way upstairs to the second story, where I found a nice secluded spot to finish reading my book.

I'll admit, I was slightly disappointed when I came in and Sebastian was nowhere in sight, even though I told myself that I'd gone there to see the books, not particularly him. But when I looked up from my reading and found him watching me, quite similar to the way he'd caught me watching him the week before, a shiver of excitement ran up my spine.

And then when he told me he wanted to see me again...

"What's got you over there smiling like that?"

"Huh?" I said, looking up from my food. "Oh, I'm just excited that we're going to be working together again."

"Carmen Jones, don't sit there and lie to me," Heather said. Her mouth drew up into a grin as she asked, "What's his name?"

There was no use in keeping it a secret, so I went on to tell her about Sebastian. I told her about our encounter less than an hour ago when he'd asked me out. I left out the part where I almost fell on my face in front of him.

"He told me to ask for that at the bar," I said, as I handed her the card I'd shoved into the back pocket of my jeans before taking off to meet her for lunch.

"Hemingway?" she said, looking just as confused as I'd felt when I first read it.

"Yeah, I don't know," I said, shrugging as I picked my fork up to begin eating again. "Maybe it's a drink on a secret menu or something."

"Maybe," Heather murmured, flipping the card over to the front. "Hey Carmen, what did you say Sexy Reader's name was again?"

"Sebastian Kincaid," I said, chewing my food.

"As in...*Owner* of By the Books Bookstore?"

My fork fell from my hands, and my head flew up to meet her eyes.

"What?" I said, reaching over to snatch the card back and really look at it for the first time. Sure enough, his name was embossed on the front, underneath of the name of the bookstore.

"You didn't know?" Heather asked.

"No," I said. "I just thought he worked there. When he gave me the card, I was too busy looking at and wondering what the hell Hemingway meant. I hadn't even looked at the other side until right now."

"Wow," Heather said, shaking her head as she pulled out her phone.

"What are you doing?" I asked, as she quickly pecked away on her phone.

"I'm looking him up, duh," she said, and a moment later she shouted, "Damn!" so loud that several other customers turned and looked in our direction. "Is that him?" she asked, pushing her phone across the table toward me.

I looked down at the photo on the screen, and my body reacted to it as if he were standing right in front of me; those chocolate pools staring at me beneath long eyelashes. I nodded and Heather took her phone back to look at his picture again.

"Homeboy is beyond fione!" she exclaimed, causing me to giggle at her exaggeration on the word fine. "And he's successful, by owning a bookstore, which is like your fortress of solitude."

"I know," was all I could say.

"What are you wearing Saturday night?"

"I have no idea," I said. "Why don't you come over and help me?" It had been way too long since we'd hung out at one of our places.

Heather seemed to love the idea as she smiled and nodded.

"We're gonna have Mr. Sexy *Bookstore Owner* drooling when sees you on Saturday night," Heather said with a wink.

I couldn't wait.

CHAPTER FIVE

M y ride share driver was extremely chatty, so when she parked her car in front of By the Books, I quickly hit 'pay' on the app on my phone and hopped out. She was a sweet older lady, who'd asked so many questions. Her questions just made me more nervous the closer we got to the destination.

I hadn't dated in a *really* long time. So even though I was excited, I was also a bit on edge.

But she did compliment me on my dress when I first got in. After she drove off once I got out of the car, I ran my hands down the red bell sleeved dress with scoop back that stopped mid-thigh. It hugged my body to perfection, showing off my curves just enough.

I blew out a breath and ran a quick hand through my hair before taking a step forward toward the door of the bookstore. I was surprised to see how full the place was considering the time of the evening.

But the vibe in the evening was completely different from the one during the day. The day crowd seemed to be more laid-back and quiet. But now, the bar was filled with people enjoying, what I assumed were drinks from the 'evening' menu. The people now seemed livelier, all the different conversations blending together to create an energetic hum.

I made my way over to the bar where the woman who'd made my iced coffee several days ago, was topping off a drink with whipped cream after she'd poured a splash of amaretto liqueur into it.

"What can I get for you?" she asked, as she pushed the drink in front of a customer and took their credit card to pay for the drink.

"I..." I squeezed my way through a couple of people to get closer to the bar. "I'm looking for Sebastian," I said, raising my voice slightly so she could hear me.

"You and half the women in here, honey," she said as she punched the touchscreen a few times before swiping the credit card. She turned back toward the bar, handing the customer next to me their card back, along with a receipt. They stuffed some cash in the tip jar, after signing the receipt and she smiled and nodded at them. Once the customer moved away from the bar, I took the vacant spot.

"I'm supposed to be meeting him," I said, growing slightly annoyed. "He told me to ask for a Hemingway."

At that word, she stopped what she was doing and looked up at me, her face splitting into a wide grin.

"So, you're her," she said, eyeing me from head to toe, before nodding in what seemed to be approval. Then she turned to one of the other bartenders and whispered something in his ear. He nodded and she motioned for me to follow her as she came from around the bar.

"I'm Suzette, by the way," she said, introducing herself.

"Carmen," I replied slowly. I looked around confused as we headed down an aisle towards the back of the bookstore.

I couldn't contain the gasp when she reached up and tipped a book on the shelf against the wall back and one of the bookcases *actually* shifted, revealing a set of stairs that led down to a basement.

I turned to the woman and frowned at her.

"He's not some serial killer, down there waiting for me to show up so he can chop me up into little pieces, is he?" I asked.

"*What?*" Suzette screeched and then laughed. "No. Have you never been down there before?"

"I've only been here twice," I said. "I wasn't aware of this store two weeks ago, let alone the fact that there was anything in the basement worth seeing."

"Well then you're in for a real treat," she said, and opened the door wider.

"Okay," I said, before turning toward the door.

It was all so mysterious, I thought to myself as I made my way down the dimly lit winding staircase. I'd now figured out that 'Hemingway' was obviously some kind of password for whatever was down in the basement. But *what* was down there?

Jazz music began to fill my ears, and the further down I went, the louder it became. I heard a knock on a door, followed by a sliding sound.

I heard a voice say the same password I'd given Suzette, followed by another sliding sound and finally the unlocking of a door.

When I reached the bottom of the stairs, I came face to face with a big burly man standing in front of a door where the music was obviously coming from, as well as two women dressed clearly ready to have a good time. I assumed that they'd come down the alley staircase from outside.

The huge guy opened the door behind him and stepped

to the side. He looked at me, but didn't say anything, so I figured that he assumed I'd given someone the password in the bookstore and was good to go. The women scurried inside and I followed them in.

I was...speechless.

Hidden underneath the bookstore, was a speakeasy-type club. And it was full of people at the bar and at tables, listening to the live band on stage while enjoying their drinks. I turned in a slow circle, taking in everything around me in awe.

I froze when my eyes locked with Sebastian's.

He was heading in my direction, his gait easy and smooth as his eyes caressed my body from head to toe. I was thankful for the low lighting and I hoped he wouldn't be able to see the blush from the open appreciation I found in his gaze.

"Welcome to 154," he said. "It's nice to see you again, Carmen Jones."

"And it's nice to see you as well," I said. I looked around before my eyes met his again. "This is amazing, Sebastian."

"I'm glad you like it," he said, his lip curving up into a proud grin. He turned and placed his hand on my lower back to gently guide me further into the club. He led me over to a table that was off to the side, but had a good view of the stage.

He held a chair out for me and once I was seated, he took the chair next to me, forcing me to turn to see him.

"You look stunning," he said, once he was seated.

"And you look exactly like the *owner* I had no idea you were until I finally took the time to look at your business card."

The last two times I'd seen Sebastian, he'd been dressed down in a black T-shirt and jeans. But tonight, he looked damn good in a charcoal grey suit, slim black tie and cognac colored wing-tipped boots.

The man wore the hell out of a suit and he looked absolutely delicious.

He chuckled and slid his arm across the back of my chair as he asked, "That didn't change your opinion of me in any way, did it?"

I knew what he was trying to politely ask. He was curious as to whether I was more attracted to him now that I knew he owned the place and wasn't just an employee there. I quickly put his mind at ease, when I shook my head and replied in a tone that should have brooked no doubt, "Not at all."

He studied me for a moment, and then nodded. He turned, lifted his hand and a waiter was at our table seconds later. He took our drink orders and then hurried off.

"They sure do know how to come when the boss summons them, don't they?" I teased.

Sebastian smiled, and that dimple that I found myself wanting to dip my tongue into revealed itself.

He shook his head and said, "Just good service is all that is. I'm off the clock tonight, enjoying good jazz, great food and drinks with even greater company."

I smiled and looked away, finally looking down at the limited menu. While it didn't have a ton of food options, that didn't negate it from having some tantalizing choices. The waiter returned with our drinks and took our orders.

Once he was gone, I looked up at Sebastian and said, "So, a bookstore with a hidden club underground. It's very 1920s."

He set his glass of Hennessy on the rocks down before answering, "That was the idea."

"And how did you come up with it?"

Sebastian shrugged. "Watching too many gangster movies involving prohibition as a kid I guess. I found the secrecy of it all fascinating and always wanted to open one someday. Even when I went to college, the desire never went away."

"Why a bookstore as the 'front'?" I asked, holding up my fingers to make air quotes.

"I love books," he said simply. "So much so that it's what I have my degree in."

"Literature?"

He nodded and added, "Master's."

"Nice," I said, genuinely impressed. "And where did you get your degrees?"

"Oxford."

"Excuse me," I said, laughing. "Oxford University? As in Oxford, England? In the United Kingdom?"

He smiled as he said, "That's the only one I know of. You seem incredibly surprised."

"I am, and yet you seem so chill about it."

"It's just another college," he said.

"I find that very hard to believe," I said.

"What? I applied there, just like anyone else. There were a few things different in the process, but at the end of the day, I was accepted."

"What made you decide to go there rather than stay here in the states?"

"I guess it was an opportunity to see another part of the world. And I received a Rhodes Scholarship for the graduate program, so it wasn't hard to decide to stay–"

"Whoa, whoa, whoa!" I said, holding up my hands to stop him. "You went to one of the world's most impressive universities *and then* you received one of the most prestigious scholarships in the world. And you're just sitting here like we're discussing some basic shit, like the weather."

"I really don't know what to tell you," he said, and I found his humbleness extremely cute.

"For a black man to have accomplished so much," I said, shaking my head. "It couldn't have been easy to be there alone. And I don't imagine there were a lot of people there who looked like you."

My last comment caused him to laugh. "That's for sure," he said. "When I found another person, who looked like me, you better believe we became inseparable."

"Was he from America too?" I asked, completely intrigued by his story.

Sebastian shook his head and picked his glass up. "He was from the UK."

"Do the two of you still keep in touch since you've been back in the states?"

"Actually–"

"I became his business partner."

I looked up to find another handsome man staring down at us with a mischievous grin on his lips.

His skin was dark and smooth and he reminded me of a certain famous black British actor that the women tended to go crazy over. I had no doubt this man had the same 'problem'.

"I see living in the United Kingdom all those years didn't teach you any manners, Bas," he teased.

Sebastian rolled his eyes, before making the introductions. "Carmen Jones, this is Reilly Lawrence. Rye, this is Carmen."

Reilly reached his hand across the table toward me and when I placed my hand in his, he bowed slightly. "It is a pleasure to meet you, Carmen," he said, and then kissed my hand.

"Rye," I heard Sebastian gnarl next to me. I found the hint of jealousy radiating from him slightly arousing for some odd reason.

Reilly chuckled – obviously amused that he'd gotten a rise out of Sebastian – and then released my hand.

"It's nice to meet you too," I said, tickled by the fact that Sebastian was annoyed with his flirtatious friend.

"You know," Reilly started. "I don't think ol' Bas here has ever brought a lady in here as his personal guest."

"Don't you have work to do?" Sebastian asked, narrowing his eyes.

Reilly held up his hands and said, "Indeed I do. You two enjoy your evening."

"He seems nice," I said, as Reilly walked away. "So, he moved to the states and you two became business partners?"

"Not right away," Sebastian said. "Rye was working in finance and I was trying my hand at high school teaching. Wasn't quite my thing, so eventually I came back to my original dream."

"Wow," I said.

The waiter finally brought our food, and I opened my mouth to ask another question, but Sebastian cut me off. "We've talked about me *way* too much for one evening," he said, smiling. "How is everything going with Bobby and his book deal?"

I returned his smile and said, "Things are great actually. He should be getting his royalty check soon." I'd received my cut from it just this morning. It was quite a satisfying thing to wake to seeing it in my bank account. "Next, we'll start shopping the book to movie studios."

"That's great," Sebastian said. "I can't imagine someone more deserving of success than Bobby."

"He is one of the nicest people I've met," I agreed. "And Ellie is just the sweetest."

"She is."

We began eating. The food was amazing, like everything else in this place, including the man sitting next to me.

"Is Bobby your only client?" Sebastian asked, after we'd sat in silence for a while.

"He was until his deal went through," I said. "Now my phone's been ringing nonstop. Quite a few of my old clients seem to be crawling back."

"As they should," Sebastian said. "Seems like they've realized how much they took you for granted. Clearly they didn't realize how valuable you were."

"No, they didn't."

"Are you taking them back up as clients?"

"Some, not all. I've also had potential new clients calling lately. It's going to be nice to have some freshness on my roster."

"It sounds like your solo venture is going to be a success."

I sat up a little higher as pride bloomed in my chest and said, "It is going to be."

"Attagirl," he said, holding up his glass, sending a toast my way.

We continued our meal in relative silence. We were just finishing up when the live band completed their set.

"They were great," I said, leaning over to say in Sebastian's ear.

"They come in a couple of nights a week," he said. "They're not the main event though."

"Really?" I asked.

"No, it's actually spoken word open mic night," he said.

"That is so cool," I said excitedly.

"Yeah, we have a few regulars that come in and spit some really good shit. It's never boring, that's for sure."

I settled in next to Sebastian, who'd once again, draped his arm over the back of my chair. We weren't sitting too close to each other, but I could definitely feel his body heat radiating next to me.

And it was turning me on slightly.

Okay, maybe a *little* more than slightly.

Who am I kidding? The man had me ridiculously horny, from his presence alone.

The waiter came and cleared our table and asked, "Are you interested in any dessert?"

Sebastian looked at me and I politely shook my head.

"Hey boss man," the waiter said, turning to Sebastian. "You gettin' on stage tonight?"

I felt Sebastian stiffen slightly, and he ran his hand against the back of his neck as he gave an apprehensive smile.

"Hadn't planned on it," he said.

"Ah man," the waiter complained. "Come on, you have to. You always get things lit up in here."

"I'm kind of in the middle of something right now," Sebastian said, trying to evade the situation.

"I don't mind," I spoke up quickly.

Sebastian turned to look me in the eyes and I smiled.

"There's no way I'm going to let this slide," I teased. "I *have* to hear this."

Sebastian sighed and removed his arm from behind me. I missed the contact probably way more than I should have for a first date. He stood, undid the buttons on his suit jacket, revealing a vest in a matching color underneath. He took off his jacket, and draped it over the back of his own chair. He then loosened his tie, and reached for the cufflinks at his wrists. He tucked the expensive looking pieces into his pockets and then rolled up his sleeves.

I couldn't help but squirm in my seat as I watched him. He never took his eyes from mine, and my mind drifted to what it would be like watching him remove *all* his clothes.

He bent down slightly so that he was looking me right in the eyes.

"Just a forewarning, you may feel a bit more...stimulated by the time I'm done."

I took in a gulp of air, refraining from telling him that I was already probably as stimulated as I could get where he was concerned.

I quickly learned just how wrong I was, after the waiter went on stage to introduce Sebastian and then he stepped up to the mic and began to speak.

CHAPTER SIX

Sebastian

"She opens for me
    At the slightest touch, the gentlest caress
    She opens wide for me
    She reveals things to me I never imagined I'd discover
    Deep inside of her
    I get lost
    In new worlds and old ones too
    She opens for me
    And the deeper I go, the higher I end up
    Every time she opens wide
    It always feels like the first time
    I never get tired of her
    And she always opens for me."

When I was finished, I finally opened my eyes to the raucous applause from the crowd. My eyes went directly to Carmen, who was on her feet clapping with the rest of the audience. And just as I'd warned her beforehand, I could tell she was even more aroused than I'd sensed she had been before I got on stage. From the conversation we'd had earlier as I divulged my background, I could tell one of the things she got off on was intelligence.

I left the stage and made my way back over to her. The closer I got to her, the more I zeroed in on her heated cheeks and the subtle outline of her hardened nipples beneath her dress. The sight made my mouth water.

When I got back to the table, we both sat and the waiter was just placing a fresh round of drinks on the table for us. He gave me a pat on the back as he said, "I told you that you'd get it started up in here. That was dope."

"Thanks, man," I said, giving him a short nod, before grabbing my glass and tossing back the cognac.

I *really* had no intention of performing anything. Had no desire to tonight. But I couldn't say no when Carmen insisted.

"That was..." Carmen shook her head. "Incredibly hot. Did you write that yourself?"

I nodded, taking another sip. "I did."

She leaned into me and whispered in my ear, "So, was that about your passion for a woman or your passion for books?"

For some reason, my dick twitched at the fact that she'd picked up on the double entendre of the poem. I leaned closer to her and our lips were a mere brush a way from each other's as I said, "It's subjective to the listener."

She let out a sexy little breath, and licked her lips, before sitting back.

"Now that I've been thoroughly put on the spot, I think it's time I get to know a little more about you."

"What would you like to know?" she asked, grabbing her glass that was filled with an apple martini.

"Your name for starters. Was that just a coincidence or were you named after the movie character?"

"The character," Carmen admitted. "My mother was obsessed with Dorothy Dandridge. She practically wanted to be the woman."

"Are you two close?" I asked.

Carmen's shoulders grew rigid as she shook her head and brought her glass to her lips. "Unfortunately, she and Dorothy had a little too much in common. She died of an accidental overdose when I was fifteen."

I watched as Carmen finished off her drink in one large gulp.

"I'm sorry," I said, gently. "I didn't mean to bring up bad memories."

Carmen shook her head. "It's fine. It was a long time ago. My dad and stepmom raised me. I don't think I turned out too bad," she said with a grin.

"Not bad at all," I said, returning her grin. "So, I know you're this hotshot literary agent climbing your way back to the top. Where did you go to college?"

"I majored in literature as well," she started, smiling. "I graduated from Stanford."

I threw my head back and laughed. "Wait a damn minute," I said. "You've been over there fawning over how I went to Oxford–"

"I wouldn't say I was *fawning*," she attempted to deny.

I continued right on talking as if she hadn't just spoken. "And your ass is a *Stanford* grad?"

She grinned sheepishly as she threw my own words back at me. "It's just another college."

"Right," I said, finishing off my drink, my lip curling up. "Now, you want to act all bashful."

"Whatever," she said, rolling her eyes.

"What made you want to become a literary agent?" I asked, deciding to chill on messing with her.

That question made her light up again.

"The short and succinct answer to that question is basically the same reason why you chose to open a bookstore. Simply put, I love books."

I totally understood that, of course. She was clearly a woman after my own heart. "I dig that," I said with a nod. "What happens when you stumble across a book that's not up to par?"

Carmen scrunched her nose and shook her head. "That's one of the things I *hate* about my job. I try my best to let those authors down gently. Even though the book may not be the best, they've still put in time and effort to write a book. Usually I send a letter, informing that, regrettably, their work isn't quite what we're looking for now."

"What if the book has potential?"

"Then I tell them that. And I put them in touch with the right people who can help them work on the book to, hopefully, make it into a good one."

"And then there are the actual good ones," I said.

"Yes," she said. "For them, I shop their books around to publishers. And I don't stop until I have a deal for my client. Which I'm sure is how I earned the title 'Cut-Throat Carmen'."

"'Cut-Throat Carmen', huh?" I repeated. "I can see that. You clearly look like the type who doesn't take shit from anyone."

"I don't," she said.

She had a take-charge aura about her that I found incredibly sexy.

The waiter came back on stage to announce the next poet and we turned to focus on the performer.

Well, I *tried* to focus on the performer. I was much more interested in the woman sitting next to me. The things we had in common fascinated me and I was eager to learn more about her.

I glanced at her through my peripheral and noticed the way she gave her attention to the performance. Occasionally, I'd feel her gaze on me, but the moment I shifted to look at her, she quickly turned away.

Several more artists performed and soon it was closing time.

"I should order a car to pick me up," she said, pulling out her phone. When she was finished, I stood and pulled out her chair for her to stand.

"We can wait upstairs," I suggested.

Carmen nodded, and we made our way to the entrance. I said good night to our bouncer and while the rest of the crowd headed toward the exit that would take them directly outside, we went to the stairs that led back up to the bookstore.

"I have to say, coming down here, through a door that's masked as a bookcase, is pretty damn neat."

I smiled, remembering when the idea had come to me.

"I figured people would get a kick out of it."

We reached the top of the stairs and I pushed the button to open the door so we could go through the bookstore, which had closed about an hour ago. We were passing by the hall that led to the back of the store, which included my office, when I stopped her by gently grabbing her elbow.

"I have something for you," I said.

"Really?" she asked, looking confused.

"Yeah,"

I pulled out my keys, unlocked my office door and turned on the light as I walked in. I went over and opened my desk drawer.

"I believe this belongs to you," I said, pulling out her book she'd left the last time she'd visited.

Carmen's eyes grew wide and she stepped further into my office. I'd noticed the way she'd curiously inspected the space, with an impressed look on her face.

"So *this* is where I left it," she said.

I nodded, looking down as I flipped through the pages.

"I've gotta say, Ian and Giselle were an interesting couple."

"You read it?" she gasped.

I handed her back her book, a grin on my face as I did so.

Our fingers brushed against each other as she took the book back, and the jolt from the contact hit me right in the groin.

I could tell she felt something too. She pulled her lip between her teeth and held up the book, a smug look on her face as she said, "I thought you said you didn't see yourself as 'one of those guys' who read romance novels."

"Well, you were the one who said to give it a shot," I threw back at her.

"And? What did you think about it?"

I blew out a breath and shoved my hands in my pockets. "Honestly," I said. "It was pretty fuckin' hot."

After sneaking a peek at the page she'd bookmarked, I found myself flipping to the beginning. I only intended to glaze over a chapter or two, just to see what the hell the fuss was about. It seemed like I blinked and I was half way through the damn thing, and completely invested in the characters.

"You do know this was book two in a four-book series," she said. "So now you gotta go back and read the first one. And then you have to read the two after this one."

I shook my head and chuckled. "We'll see," I said, as I came back around my desk. I turned the light back off, shut the door and locked it before we continued to the front of the store.

Her car had just pulled up when we made it to the front door.

"Shit," she said, as we looked outside at the rain coming down. It was light but still nothing you'd want to get caught in.

I reached over to the bin next to the door that held several umbrellas and grabbed one. After opening the door for Carmen, I hit the release button on the umbrella and held it up for her so she wouldn't get wet.

"Seems like you're always prepared, Sebastian Kincaid," Carmen said with a grin.

"I try," I replied.

But honestly, I wasn't prepared for the affect Carmen had on me. Especially tonight when she'd walked into the club. I'd seen her in business attire and I'd seen her in a simple shirt and jeans. But when she'd sauntered into the club in that sexy red dress, showing off her legs that went on for days and that svelte body, I had to take a moment to get myself under control.

The desire that had been sparked was overwhelming.

Carmen turned to face me under the umbrella and looked up at me.

"I had a great time tonight," she said.

"So did I."

She rose on her toes and pressed her soft lips to my cheek and let them linger there. She'd slowly pulled away and began to turn for the car, when I wrapped my hand around her wrist and gently tugged her back toward me.

She came back willingly and looked up at me with

expectant eyes. I reached up and slid my hand to the back of her neck and her eyes drifted closed. I tilted her head back and leaned down, tentatively pressing my lips to hers. When she sank against me, confirming that she'd wanted this just as much as I did, I deepened the kiss, letting my hand slide from her neck all the way down to the top of her ass, bringing her body even closer to mine. I gave her backside a gentle squeeze as my tongue slid across the seam of her mouth. She opened for me, and when our tongues touched, I gripped the handled on the umbrella just a little bit tighter.

While I could have gone on kissing her in the rain under the umbrella, I knew that her driver was waiting for her. So I reluctantly pulled away, but not before taking one last nibble of her sweet lips.

Her eyes finally fluttered open, looking as dazed as I felt from the kiss.

"Shoot me a text when you get home," I said, releasing my grip on her. "My number is on the card I gave you."

She nodded and I reached around her to open the door for her. I moved with her, keeping the umbrella over her until she was safely in the car.

"Good night, Sebastian," she said, looking up at me.

"Good night," I replied.

I closed the door and watched the car drive away, eager for the next chance to see Carmen again.

CHAPTER SEVEN

Sebastian

I looked up at the knock on my open office door and saw Reilly walking in. It was Monday, my usual day to do all the mundane work for the bookstore, like the annoying paperwork. Reilly dropped down in the chair across from me as I finished up the order I was working on. He leaned back and kicked his feet up onto my desk, crossing one ankle over the other and I promptly shoved them off.

"What is it, Rye?" I asked, finally looking up.

"You're really gonna make me ask?" Reilly said, sitting up.

"Ask what?"

"How did things go Saturday night?"

I shook my head. "You were there, Rye. You saw it for yourself."

"I'm talkin' about *after* you left the club," he said, wiggling his eyebrows.

I chuckled and sat back in my chair. "I hate to burst your nosey ass bubble, but nothing happened."

"Bollocks!" he shouted.

"It's the truth," I exclaimed. "She ordered a car, I walked her out, and we said goodbye. That's it."

"That's it?" Reilly repeated.

I shrugged as I sat back up and began to get back to work.

"You didn't even kiss her goodnight?"

My fingers slowed briefly on the keyboard, and my mind drifted back to the way I felt having Carmen's body pressed against mine.

"There it is!" Reilly said, laughing.

"Shut up," I said, shaking my head.

"She was gorgeous, mate."

"Yeah."

"When are you gonna see her again?" Reilly asked.

"Soon I hope."

When Reilly didn't say anything for a minute, I looked up to find him studying me.

"What?" I huffed, annoyed by his scrutiny.

"You really fancy this girl, don't you?"

Knowing I wasn't going to get any work done until Reilly got the hell out of my office, I sat back in my chair again.

"Yeah, I really like her," I said. "She's different. She's like...me."

"Meaning, she ain't like some of the daft birds you've gone out with before?"

Those relationships had never lasted long. They'd all been missing the substance that I craved. Even the intelligent women that I'd gone out with lacked something; a spark, I guess.

Carmen Jones definitely had plenty of spark.

"That's exactly what it means," I said.

Seeming to finally be satisfied with my answers, Reilly tapped the arms of the chairs and then stood.

"Well, just make sure you don't cock it up, eh?"

"Cock it–" I shook my head. Even after all of these years of knowing Reilly, some of his slang still threw me for a loop, no matter how many times I'd heard it. "Rye, I'm not gonna screw anything up," I said.

Reilly nodded and then turned to head for the door.

After he was gone, I tried to get back to work, but there was no use. I couldn't stop thinking about Carmen.

I looked down at my phone sitting on my desk. I had her number stored in my phone after she'd texted me to let me know she'd made it home safely. I grabbed it, and scrolled through my contacts until I found her name.

Then I sat back and thought about what I wanted to text. It had to be something cool, while not coming on too strong, too fast.

After a few minutes, I began typing out a message.

I kept my expression cool as the publishing company executive I was sitting in front of shook his head. I was in the middle of a meeting for one of my new clients.

"Carmen–"

"I don't understand how this is even an issue," I said, cutting him off. "This author has *consistently* written hit after hit for you. Yet you're sitting there acting like an increased advance to renew his contract is something completely unheard of."

"I didn't say it was unheard of, it's just–"

"You're trying to lock him in with a five-book deal. *Five* books! Yet you don't want to make it worth his while?" I shook my head, and grabbed my purse before standing. "You know what? Forget about it. I know at least three other publishers who have been chomping at the bit, just waiting for him to finish his contract with you so they can swoop in. Maybe I should go and hear what they have to say."

I was already turning to head for the door when I heard, "Wait!"

My lip tilted up slightly, before I turned back to him. My eyebrow quirked up as I waited.

"I can do a five–"

I turned again for the door, when he shouted, "Ten! I can increase his next advance by ten percent. That's the best I can do, Carmen."

"We look forward to continuing my client's business with you," I said, before opening the office door and walking out.

I reached into my purse and pulled out my phone, and smiled at the text on my phone.

Sebastian: Working hard?

I hit the button on the elevator and as I waited for the car to reach my floor, I typed out a response.

'Cut-Throat Carmen' strikes again!

The elevator pinged at the exact same time that my phone buzzed. I read Sebastian's response as I entered the elevator.

Sebastian: That's awesome. Sounds like you could use a celebratory drink.

Are you offering? I texted, eager for his reply.

Sebastian: Yeah, I am. Why don't you come by the bookstore?

"Going down?"

I looked up and realized I wasn't alone on the elevator.

"Uh, yes. First floor, please," I said, looking back down at my phone so I could text Sebastian back.

I'll see you in about fifteen minutes.

It was late afternoon when I arrived at By the Books. There weren't many people there, just a few milling around the bookstore, while a few others were sitting at tables working on their laptops.

I'd sent Sebastian a text when I arrived and he responded that he'd be out in a few minutes. He told me to grab a seat and he'd find me, so I went to what had instantly become my favorite spot in the bookstore, the small little alcove on the second floor.

I was just finishing up with a text when I looked up and saw Sebastian heading my way, holding two shot glasses.

"Are these the celebratory drinks you mentioned?" I asked as I stood and smiled.

"They sure are," Sebastian said as he stopped in front of me and handed me a drink.

"It's a little early for shots, isn't it?" I asked. "I expected a coffee or something."

"You know the saying, 'It's five o'clock somewhere,'" he said with dancing eyes.

He bent down to kiss my cheek. The flutters in my stomach kicked up instantly at the feel of his lips on my skin. The memory of the kiss we'd shared two nights ago came rushing back.

He pulled away and held up his glass.

"To 'Cut-Throat Carmen' striking again," he said, causing me to laugh out loud. I covered my mouth, not wanting to disturb anyone and then clinked my glass against his.

I drank the shot, squinting and watched as Sebastian made a similar face.

"What is *in* that?" I asked, rubbing my chest as the heat from the liquor began to bloom there.

Sebastian shook his head. "Honestly, I don't know. I had Suzette make it, told her to call it the 'Cut-Throat'."

I laughed again and said, "Well she did the name justice, that's for sure."

We set the glasses down on the table and then sat down across from each other.

"How's work going for you today?" I asked.

"Slow," he said. "Especially when Rye was in my office earlier getting on my damn nerves."

"I think it's really cool that the two of you were able to stay friends and are now working together," I said.

"He's my brother."

I totally believed it. Just witnessing the dynamic between them briefly when Reilly introduced himself, I could tell that they were close.

"Do you have any actual siblings?" I asked, curious to know more about him.

"An older sister," he said. "She's married with two kids. They live in California."

"Really? My dad and stepmom live out there."

"So, is that where you're from?" he asked.

"No, he was offered a job out there when I was in college. The pay was great, so he took it. He always wanted to live by the ocean. He's retired now."

"Do you get out there to visit often?"

"Not as often as I should," I said, feeling slightly guilty.

"Yeah, I don't get to see my sister that much either. My nieces are getting so big."

He reached into his pocket and pulled out his phone and after scrolling a minute he passed it to me.

"That's Ava," he said pointing at the younger one. "She's three. And Miss Snaggletooth there is Aria. She's six."

"They're adorable," I gushed, looking down at the two little girls with pigtails – one missing her front teeth – smiling brightly in the photo.

I handed the phone back to Sebastian, who grinned down at the picture, before shoving his phone back in his pocket. "Yeah, they are."

"You look like the ultimate proud uncle," I said.

"Tell me about your day," Sebastian said, sitting back in his chair.

I told him about the contract renewal deal I'd just made before coming over to the bookstore. I even rambled on about some of the mundane things about my day. Not once did he ever seem bored. He was extremely attentive, commenting and even asking questions.

Before I knew it, nearly two hours had gone by. The pinging of Sebastian's phone interrupted us.

"Shit, it's Suzette texting me from downstairs," he said, reading the text. "They're starting to get swamped with the evening crowd."

"Go," I insisted. "I've taken up way too much of your time as it is."

"I'm not complaining one bit," he said, standing. I stood as well and was pleasantly surprised when he came around the table and pulled me into his arms. "I'm not going downstairs until I get you to agree to go on another date with me."

His words made me smile. His hands resting on my hips made me want to push my body even closer to his.

"Yes," was all I said, but it was enough to make that dimple in his cheek appear. He leaned down and gently pressed his lips towards mine, and this time I actually did move in closer, until there was no space between us. I slid my arms around his shoulders and my fingers grazed the fine hairs on the nape of his neck.

I'd just opened my mouth to invite his tongue in when we heard, "*Sebastian!*" being shouted from downstairs.

He slowly ended the kiss, pressing his forehead to mine as he said, "She forgets who's running things around here. That's what happens when you hire your family to work for you."

"You'd better get down there," I said, reluctant to let him go.

He nodded and finally pulled away. I grabbed my purse and he walked me back downstairs and to the front door.

"I'll call you later, or tomorrow so we can set something up."

"Okay," I said, and then left the bookstore.

CHAPTER EIGHT

"Carmen, at the rate you're going, you're going to need to hire another agent. Maybe even two. The queries you have coming in daily is through the roof."

I looked over at Heather who was sitting on the floor next to me in front of my laptop. We were combing through my emails trying to get things organized. While I'd had plenty of calls, emails and letters inquiring about my services, so far I'd only taken on one other person as a client. While both contracts were locked down, Bobby was keeping me busy, as we were getting ready to begin work with the publishing company on shopping the book around to production studios to sell the movie rights of his book series. So I was taking my time on accepting new clients. Just because the requests were suddenly rolling in, didn't mean I was accepting all of them.

I still had my same standards, and if it didn't feel right, I wasn't going for it. There were some people that I already knew wouldn't be a good fit for my business, while there were others I was still trying to feel out.

I'd worked with nearly fifty clients at my old job, and I

had no doubt that I'd build my roster back up to that number, if not more. And one of the ways I intended to get some new clients was by attending a writers' convention. Heather was taking care of the registration.

"If you'd have kept going to these conferences over the last year, like *I told you to,* you would have already been able to hire me," she playfully chastised, bumping me with her shoulder before she went back to helping me set up my travel plans. We'd moved on from the emails after going through and deciding which ones were actually worth my time.

"The only reason I haven't officially hired you now," I said, "is because I want to make sure the health insurance is in place."

"And I appreciate that," Heather said.

With Heather being a single mom to Tevin, she couldn't afford not to have health insurance. Especially when her son was quite rambunctious. I absolutely couldn't steal her away until everything was set up just right. Of course, she was helping me with that portion of the business as well. I would truly be lost on that side of things without her. I offered to pay her, even though she wasn't officially my employee yet, but she refused. She said that for now, she was just 'helping out a friend'. Since she refused my money, I'd slipped Tevin a little something when they first arrived. It had gotten me a serious side-eye from Heather, but she didn't make him give it back.

"Aunt Carmen!"

The adorable boy, who was the spitting image of his late father, came rushing over, but froze at his mother's glare and the finger she pointed at him.

"Boy, what have I told you about running through people's houses?" she said sternly.

"Sorry, Aunt Carmen," Tevin said, hanging his hand in shame.

"It's okay," I said with a smile. I didn't mind his energetic nature, but Heather had her rules with her son and I wouldn't dare undermine them. So I tacked on a, "Just don't let it happen again."

He nodded and said, "Yes ma'am."

"What did you need, sweetie?" I asked.

"Can I get something to eat out of the kitchen?"

Heather let out an exasperated huff. "You ate before we got here."

"I'm hungry again," Tevin whined.

"It's fine with me, as long as your mother says yes."

We both turned to Heather. She looked from Tevin to me, and I made sure to turn on the puppy dog look in Tevin's favor. Finally, she waved her hand and said, "Make sure you wash your hands, and leave Aunt Carmen's kitchen the way you found it!"

Tevin smiled, turned and began to run, but then thought better of it and walked quickly to the kitchen.

Heather shook her head, as she turned back to the computer. "You spoil him."

"What?" I laughed. "The boy was hungry."

"He's *always* hungry."

Heather looked over her shoulder and then back to me before she whispered, "He's been asking for a sibling lately."

"What?" I shrieked, only to have Heather shush me.

"I know." Heather shook her head again as she went back to typing. "I've been evasive when he brings it up. But, what am I supposed to say to a ten-year-old? 'Hey son, I know you want a baby brother or sister, but that's kind of hard when you're a twenty-nine-year-old single mother of a ten-year-old. Men generally don't find that attractive.'"

"Heather–" I tried to soothe, but she cut me off.

"You know it's true Carmen. When guys find out I have a son, they act like I have the plague."

"Because those guys are losers. You'll find someone who doesn't mind Tevin. No, who *loves* Tevin."

"I'm not sure if I want to even bother dating anymore," Heather sighed. "But the thing is...I *want* another baby."

"Really?" This was the first time I'd ever heard her mention wanting another kid. But I could tell from the dreamy look in her eyes and the wistfulness in her voice that she was serious.

"Yes, but I don't think I can wait around for a man anymore."

"Heather?"

She nodded to my unasked question.

"I think I want to consider donors," she whispered.

"Are–are you serious?" I asked with wide eyes.

Heather's eyes narrowed as she answered, "Completely. What? Do you find something wrong with that? Plenty of women get pregnant with donors every year."

I placed my hand on her arm and gently squeezed it. "Of course I don't think there's anything *wrong* with it. I just want to make sure that you're positive that this is right for you."

"It's still just a thought," Heather said. "Would I rather do things 'the old fashion way' by meeting a good man, falling in love, all of that? Yes. But I'm being realistic. The odds are not in my favor."

"Honey, you're acting like finding love is The Hunger Games," I laughed.

"Isn't it these days? Dating is *hard*." Heather then looked over at me and grinned. "Well I guess it's not hard for you. How are things going with Mr. Sexy Bookstore Owner?"

"They're going good, we have another date this weekend. But stop trying to deflect," I insisted.

"There's nothing more to talk about, Carmen," Heather insisted. "Like I said, it's just something I'm contemplating right now. It's not like I'm ready to run off to a sperm bank and say, 'inject me with the best swimmers you have!'"

"Okay, did you have to put it like that?" I asked, and Heather laughed.

"Whatever. Okay, so you're all registered for the conference in L.A. next month. I've also arranged your travel plans. They'll show up on the app that I downloaded on your phone. Are you going to see your dad?"

"Of course," I said. "He wouldn't let me hear the end of it if I didn't. I already know he's going to complain about me staying at a hotel."

My dad had a great place out on Malibu Beach, but I decided I wanted to stay at the hotel where the conference was being held. That way I could network after the conference was done for the day. That's when you could get to know people; when their hair is down, when they loosen their ties and the drinks are in their hand.

Plus, I hadn't told him how rough the last year had been for me. I knew if I stayed with him and my stepmom, it would all come pouring out at some point. I knew I could have asked him for help with my finances and he wouldn't have hesitated to help me, but I didn't want to go there. My silly pride wouldn't let me, no matter how much of a daddy's girl I was.

"You're all set," Heather said, shutting the laptop.

"Great, and thank you again so much," I said.

"Girl, you know there's no thanks needed."

We finally stood, stretching our arms and legs and I said, "Hey, you wanna watch a movie?"

Heather looked at her watch. "It's still early, why not?" she said, shrugging. Since she always made herself at home at my place, she headed for the kitchen and said, "I'm gonna make some popcorn."

My phone pinged after she disappeared and I smiled when I saw it was a text from Sebastian.

I was still smiling and texting when Heather returned several minutes later, dropping down on the couch next to me as she shoved a handful of popcorn in her mouth.

"Ooooo, you must be texting your new booooyfriend," she sang.

"Shut up," I said, laughing. "We've only been on one date."

"Well if he's making you smile after just one date and some texts messages, you better snatch him up quick."

CHAPTER NINE

Sebastian

I punched in the code that would ring to Carmen's apartment and a few seconds later, her sexy voice came through the intercom.

"Bas?"

It was the first time she'd called me by my nickname and it sounded good.

"Yeah," I responded.

"Come on up," she said, and the door buzzed. I went in and headed for the elevator and punched the button to the tenth floor.

Carmen lived in a nice building, not much different from where I lived. Clearly, she'd done well for herself when she worked for the literary agency. I'd noticed the hurt in her eyes when she talked about her old job, it was clear she'd felt betrayed by them. But that hurt was always snuffed out with a look of determination, because she was confident that she was going to be even more successful working for herself than she ever had been with Mason and...whatever the rest of the name of that place was.

That confidence, among so many other things about her, was a major turn on.

I arrived at her floor and when I reached her door, I rang her doorbell. The door swung open and Carmen looked up at me with a bright smile.

"Hey," she said, opening the door wider so I could enter.

"Hey yourself," I said, leaning down to accept the kiss she planted on my cheek. I held up a small bouquet of flowers and then paused. "You're not allergic, are you?"

"No," she said, taking the blend of pink roses and lavender flowers in shades of purple and pink as well. "They're beautiful, Sebastian." She brought them to her nose and took a deep inhale before letting out a long, relaxed sigh.

I closed the door behind me and followed her through the apartment to the kitchen where she pulled a vase from the lower cabinet. After filling it with water, she placed the flowers into the vase.

"You've got a nice place," I said, looking around. She had a minimalistic style, clean lines. She had a mantle against one of the walls over an electric fireplace that was filled with pictures. I stopped and looked around at all the photos. There was one with her smiling with her arms wrapped around an older man, whom I assumed was her father.

"Thanks," Carmen said, coming out of the kitchen to stand next to me. My eyes landed on an older picture of a gorgeous woman with a fur wrap around, looking over her shoulder at the camera.

"Is that your mom?" I asked, turning to Carmen.

"Yep, that's her."

"You look like her."

She gave a small smile and a hint of sadness briefly crossed her face.

"I'm ready to go."

I nodded and she led the way to the door.

We were quiet as she locked her door and we walked to the elevator. When the doors shut, I finally spoke again.

"How's your week been going?"

"It's been good," she said. "I'm getting ready to steal my old secretary away from Mason and Dunn."

"No shit?" I asked, laughing. "Man, you really aren't holding anything back, are you?"

"Why should I?" Carmen asked. "After the way they treated me, when I'd made millions for them time and time again. Heather's one of my best friends. She would have left with me back then, but she had her son to think about."

"That's understandable," I said.

"She's a godsend. She's been helping me with every-thing going on. I can't wait to have her as a full-time staff member. She's already helping me stay organized and setting up travel plans for me."

"Travel plans?"

"Yeah, I'm taking a trip to L.A. soon for a writers' conference."

"L.A.?" Why did I sound like a damn parrot?

Carmen nodded. "I was going to bring it up later, during dinner."

"When is your trip?" I asked, confused by the odd feeling I felt at the thought of not being able to see her.

"Next month. It's only for a couple of days," she said, as she looked up watching the numbers tick down as we descended to the underground level of the building. She then turned to me and said, "You said your sister's in California, right?"

"Yeah, San Diego."

"You should plan a trip out there soon. I could tell that you missed her and your nieces by the way you talked about them the other day."

"You're right," I said. "Things are just so busy with work."

"You've got Reilly and Suzette there," she pointed out. "I'm sure they can manage."

"My sister is actually coming out for a visit soon. She hasn't seen the bookstore since it opened. But I'll definitely be the one to make the next trip."

"Good," Carmen said, smiling.

"So, I guess you'll be visiting your dad while you're out there?"

"Definitely," she said, still smiling as the elevator doors opened.

We walked over to my car in the visitor's parking section.

"Nice car," she said as I hit the unlock button on the key fob.

I responded with a grin as I opened her door for her. She slid in and I shut the door and went around to my side to get in. After buckling up, I started the car and drove out of the garage.

We didn't speak, allowing the music from the radio to fill the car.

The drive wasn't a long one and when we arrived at our destination, I turned to find Carmen looking at me with a grin on her face.

"Really?" she asked.

"Would you prefer we go somewhere else?"

"You're kidding, right?"

I chuckled and watched as she eagerly unbuckled her seat belt.

After we got out of the car, we walked up the steps that led to the city library.

"So, what exactly are we doing here?" she asked, curiously.

"You ever had a blind date with a book?" I asked as we entered the library.

"A what?" she laughed.

Instantly a chorus of shushes filled the room.

I shook my head and teasingly tsked at her.

"You should know better, Miss Jones," I whispered, before taking her hand and leading her over to a table. It was filled with books, all wrapped in brown parcel paper. On the front of the book were vague details about each book. Simple things like sci-fi, dystopia, romance.

"What is this?" Carmen asked.

"Basically, you pick a book. But you can't judge whether you'll enjoy reading it or not by its cover or description," I said, picking up a book and holding it up to her face. "This is all the information you get about the book."

"This is it?" she asked.

"This is it. You up for the challenge?"

She looked down at the book for a moment and then nodded. "Sure, I'm down. But I'd like to add one caveat."

"Name it."

"We have to choose the book for each other. And whatever we pick for each other, we *have* to read it."

I held out my hand and she placed hers in mine and we shook. Then I playfully tugged her hand, pulling her body against mine and stole a quick kiss.

"Let's do this," I said.

We split up and began searching through the books and

when we both picked out a book, we took them to the front desk to be checked out and then found a table in the back of the library.

We sat down and placed the books on the table in front of us.

"Are you ready?" I whispered.

"Are *you* ready?" she whispered back.

We stared at each other for a moment, and then grinned as we passed each other the books we'd chosen.

I couldn't help but chuckle when I read the description.

"Why do I get the feeling that I've been set up?" I asked, holding up the book that said 'erotica' on the brown paper.

Her face was masked in innocence as she said, "This date was *your* idea, Mister Kincaid." She looked down at her book and read the descriptions, "Femme fatale, murder mystery, noir."

"Shall we start?" I asked.

"On three?" she said, reaching for the paper wrapped around the book.

I did the same, and started the countdown. "One."

"Two."

We both said three at the same time and tore the paper off of the books, earning more shushes and side-eyes.

And then we opened our books and began to read.

Carmen

I peeked over the top of my book, which was quite enthralling, by the way. Sebastian had picked a great book for me. I kept the amused grin on my lips hidden as I watched Sebastian, clear his throat and squirm in his seat for the fifth or sixth time. I'd honestly lost count.

When his eyes slid above his own book and locked with mine, I quickly averted my gazed, attempting to focus back on my own reading. I heard Sebastian slam his book shut, before he said, "You're just loving this, aren't you?"

I covered my mouth to stifle a giggle. I didn't want any more glares of disapproval.

Before I could respond, a quiet chime filled the air, followed by a woman's hushed voice.

"The library will be closing in five minutes."

"Oh wow," I said, looking at the time on my phone. "We've been reading for two hours!" I always seemed to lose track of time when I was with Sebastian.

"I guess that announcement is our cue," Sebastian said, standing. "I didn't intend for us to stay so long."

"No, it's fine," I said. And I meant it. I'd never gone on a date where we barely talked but I still enjoyed myself. It was...comfortable.

"Are you hungry?" he asked as we walked out of the library.

"Starving."

"There's a place a couple of blocks down," Sebastian said. "They have spectacular burgers."

"A burger sounds great right now."

We opted to walk since it was still warm out, even though the sun had set some time ago.

The restaurant was full of college students, which made sense with its location being close to the library and the local university. We found an empty booth and grabbed the menus from the holder and looked over them. I hadn't realized just how hungry I was until Sebastian asked.

When the waiter came over, we placed our orders. He sat down a basket of complimentary bread and butter with a set of appetizer plates. When he left, we both reached for a roll.

"So," I said, tearing a piece of bread off before plopping it into my mouth. "How was your book?"

I was surprised when I saw his cheeks actually tint ever so slightly. He was about to respond when our waiter returned with our drinks.

Sebastian picked up his cup, and took a long drag from his straw before he pointed at me.

"That book was *nothing* like the book you left at my store," he said. "It was just...straight sex."

I threw my head back and laughed.

"Women complain about men watching porn all the time. But if *that's* the shit you all are reading, you have no room to talk about us. Y'all are just as nasty as we are."

I held my hands up in concession. "I suppose you have a point. We just like ours differently, I guess."

"Is that what you women *really* want? A good, no-strings attached fuck?"

"Some do. I certainly can't speak for all women," I said.

"Well then speak for yourself."

There was a huskiness in his tone that I hadn't heard before. When I looked into his eyes, his gaze was hungry. Now I was the one squirming in my seat and pressing my thighs tightly together.

"What do you want when it comes to sex, Carmen?" he asked.

This was my own fault, I suppose. If I hadn't have picked that damn book, we wouldn't be having this conversation. It wasn't the topic that made me uncomfortable, it was the fact that now I wanted to do exactly what we were discussing. My nipples were hard, nearly to the point of being uncomfortable, and no matter how hard I squeezed my legs, it didn't give my throbbing pussy an ounce of relief.

He was waiting for an answer and I finally gave him one.

"No, I don't particularly care for no-strings mindless fucks," I said. "I prefer a connection...intimacy."

Sebastian's lip quirked up slightly and I felt like I just might combust.

"Duly noted," he said, his voice full of promise, and the waiter picked that moment to arrive with our food.

CHAPTER TEN

Sebastian

"I had a lot of fun."

I smiled down at Carmen, who was pulling the keys out of her purse.

"So did I."

The idea of taking any other woman to the *library,* of all places, for a date never would have crossed my mind. I already knew how the date would have played out, which would have been hearing a bunch of bored complaining.

Somehow I'd known that wouldn't be the case with Carmen.

We'd spent the rest of dinner chatting about our books, Carmen more so than me. She really enjoyed her book and I enjoyed listening to her talk about it.

"Would you like to come in?"

I looked down to find Carmen gazing up at me. My eyes drifted down to her lips when her tongue came out and swiped from one side to the other.

"I wish I could," I said, taking a step closer to her. "But there's a shipment coming in at five in the morning for the club and Reilly can't be there."

"Right," Carmen said, nodding. "So, I guess this is where we say good night."

I shook my head as I lifted my hand to cup her cheek. "Not quite yet," I said, before I lowered my mouth over hers. She instantly molded her body against mine, letting out a soft little moan. I took advantage of her parting lips, tasting the inside of her sweet mouth with my tongue. My hands rested on her thick hips as I pressed her back against the door, propping my knee between her legs.

I felt my dick swell behind my zipper and I slid my hand up underneath her shirt. My hand was just about to palm her breast when the sound of loud singing brought me out of my lust-induced haze.

I pulled back and looked around, realizing we were the only two in the hallway, but the singing only got louder and louder.

"What the hell is that?" I asked.

Carmen let out a small laugh, letting her forehead drop against my chest.

"That would be my neighbor, Donnie. He's an opera singer."

"Wow, and that doesn't bother you?"

Carmen shook her head. "I enjoy it actually. He's getting ready for a show in a couple of weeks. I actually have two free tickets and I need a date."

"Are you asking me out this time?" I asked, letting my fingers continue to graze the soft skin of her waist.

"I know you're busy with your business–" she started, but I cut her off with another kiss.

"I'll make the time," I said. "Just let me know when."

"Okay," she said. She blew out a breath before looking up at me again. "Are you sure you can't come in? Not even for a cup of coffee or something?"

"I'm afraid that if I come in, I'll want more than coffee," I admitted, giving her waist a gentle squeeze. Ever since our conversation over dinner about what she preferred when it came to having sex, I couldn't stop thinking about what it'd be like to get lost between those luscious thighs.

"Next time, then," she offered.

"Next time, for sure."

Even though neither of us said the actual words, I felt like we'd both just agreed on what would happen the next time we were alone. It was inevitable. The more time I spent with Carmen, the more attracted to her and aroused I became. I wanted her, badly, even more since that chat. Nothing would stop me from having her soon enough.

What was even more arousing was that I could sense that her desire for me was just as strong as mine was for her.

Carmen finally took a step back, breaking the contact of my hand on her body, and turned to unlock her door.

"Until next time," she said, before closing the door.

I made my way to the elevator, silently cursing Reilly for deciding to pick now, of all times, to make a trip home overseas.

Carmen

I unlocked my mailbox and pulled out the pile of junk mail and looked down when I heard a key hit the floor. After closing my box, I bent down to pick up the key which had a number written on it. It was one of the keys for packages too big to fit in the normal-sized mailboxes. I went around the corner and found the designated box and opened it, finding a large envelope inside.

I couldn't tell what was inside, but I hoped some author who was a little too handy with a computer hadn't found my home address. I had a separate P.O. Box for queries and manuscripts. The last thing I needed was my mailbox constantly being flooded with that sort of thing, even though most of it came via email now.

As I walked down the hall to my condo, sifting through my mail, the scent of garlic filled my nostrils and Donatello's singing filled my ears. I stopped in front of his door and knocked. When the door swung open, the large, older Italian man smiled brightly when he saw me.

"*Ciao Bella!*" Donatello said, stepping back. "You smelled my dinner, yes?"

"Yes," I said, walking in and stopping to give him a peck on both of his cheeks. "I hope you made enough for two."

"Of course. I was going to leave some at your door. Since you're too busy to visit your old friend these days."

"Donnie–"

"No, no," he cut me off, holding up his hand. "I understand. You are the – how you say – 'hot shot' now."

I'd told him the good news about Bobby several weeks ago, but hadn't had the chance to visit him since. Donnie was like an uncle to me. He always gave sage advice and made sure I was well taken care of, which included making sure I was well fed.

"You *know* it's not like that, Donnie," I said, heading straight for the kitchen. "If anyone is the hotshot around here, it's you."

I washed my hands, grabbed a clean spoon and then lifted the top from the pot of pasta sauce Donatello had clearly made from scratch. I dipped my spoon in for a taste of the sauce and let out a satisfied moan, eager for dinner to be ready, and he shooed me out of his way. I put the spoon in the sink and grabbed my mail that I'd sat down on the island.

I grabbed the large package and ripped it open.

"What is that?" Donatello asked.

"Not sure yet," I said, reaching into the envelope to pull the contents out. When I did, I immediately rolled my eyes in annoyance at the box of expensive chocolates along with the note.

Heard you're making waves again. Congrats. We should catch up soon.
-Lee

"I know those chocolates," Donatello said, earning him a glare. Of course he'd known them. I'd shared plenty of boxes with him when Lee – my ex – used to send them on a regular basis. Now, the thought of even putting one in my mouth made me sick, or maybe it was just the thought of Lee who made me sick.

I didn't spend too much time analyzing the thoughts. I balled up the note, snatched the box up and marched over to the trash, where I dumped them.

"*Mannaggia!*" Donatello shouted. "Why did you do that, Carmen?"

"Fuck those chocolates, and fuck Lee."

"But to waste such decadence," he said in a disappointed tone.

"Aren't you currently avoiding chocolate?" Donatello always avoided anything with caffeine in it leading up to his performances. He said it dried out his vocal chords. "I'm doing you a favor," I added dryly.

Donatello shook his head, and went back to work finishing up dinner as he mumbled something in Italian, which I'm sure was about me being crazy for throwing a perfectly good box of chocolates in the trash.

But like I'd said, fuck those chocolates, and fuck Lee.

He was one of the many things I'd lost when I lost my job.

Lee Graham had been my everything for two years. We both worked at Mason and Dunn, getting hired on the same day. It was because of *me* that Lee had become so successful. But when I went down in flames, was he at my side?

Hell no!

Instead, he'd broken up with me through an email, explaining that he felt we were heading in different directions with our lives and maybe we should take some time away from each other. Which roughly translated to 'since you are unemployed, Carmen, we can't be together. Because I can't be with someone that can't support themselves.'

I had *no* intentions of 'catching up' with Lee's trifling ass.

Wanting to think of anything other than Lee, I asked Donatello, "Are you ready for opening night?"

"Of course," he said, his chest puffing out as he filled two plates with spaghetti. I filled the glasses with red wine and followed him to his dining room table. We sat and bowed our heads as Donatello said a grace over the meal in Italian before we dug in.

"I found a date to bring with me," I mumbled, before shoving another forkful of spaghetti into my mouth.

Donatello's fork clanged against his plate and he sat back and looked at me with a smile on his face.

"*È fantastico!*" he shouted and clapped his hands together. "Tell me, tell me. Who is your new young man?"

I briefly told Donatello about Sebastian over dinner and when I was finished, Donatello nodded his head.

"I cannot wait to meet him," he said. "When you talk of him, your face lights up like the moon. You like him very much, yes?"

I found myself nodding. "Yes, I do like him a lot."

After we finished eating, I thanked Donatello for dinner and then headed to my place. My cell phone was ringing when I shut the door. I pulled my phone out of my pocket and rolled my eyes when I saw the number that was, unfortunately, seared into my brain.

I hit ignore, sending it straight to voicemail.

Because...Fuck Lee!

CHAPTER ELEVEN

Sebastian

"U ncle Bas!"
I came from around the bar as my two little
nieces rushed toward me. I squatted down and caught both
Ava and Aria, in my arms for a hug. I blew raspberry kisses
on both of their cheeks, filling the bookstore with giggles.
My sister, Charlotte, was right behind them.

I stood, with a little girl in each arm, and leaned down to
kiss my big sister.

"Where's my brother-in-law?" I asked, looking around.

Charlotte let out a sigh and said, "Work. Gabe told me
to tell you he's really sorry though."

I nodded in understanding. I actually liked my sister's
husband, Gabriel, so I hated that I wouldn't get to see and
hang out with him. But I was thrilled to see my sister and
my nieces.

"Why didn't you call me?" I asked. "I would have
picked you up from the airport."

"We had a rental car reserved already," Charlotte said.

"Hey, Suzette! Look who's here."

Suzette had just come from the stockroom in the back.

She smiled and hurried over, throwing her arms around Charlotte.

"It's so good to see you, Char!" she said.

"You too," Charlotte said. "How's school?"

Suzette waved her hand. "It's school."

She turned to me and gave Ava and Aria a smile. "You two probably don't even remember me, you were teeny tiny babies when I last saw you."

"Girls," I said to them both. "This is your big cousin, Suzette."

"Would you two like some hot cocoa?" she asked. The girls responded by scrambling down and out of my arms. Suzette took their hands and looked over her shoulder at Charlotte. "Do you want anything?"

"Maybe later," Charlotte said, and Suzette nodded and headed off with the girls.

"I've got to say, little brother," Charlotte declared. "This place looks great."

"Come on," I said, wrapping my arm around her shoulder. She may have been older, but I had a good amount of height over my sister. "Let me give you a tour."

I showed her the bar, where Suzette was showing off her barista skills and making Ava and Aria giggle with delight, especially when she topped their hot cocoa off with huge dollops of whipped cream. Then I took Charlotte upstairs to look around for a bit. When we walked by the secluded little spot in the back, I instantly thought of Carmen. We'd been texting and talking on the phone almost every day.

Some days our conversations were long and deep, while other days we would just fill each other in on how our day had gone. There had even been days when one of us would refuse to get off the phone, even if we'd fallen asleep.

I enjoyed hearing her voice just that much.

We'd only gone on a few dates, but every time I saw her, I was already eager for the next time I'd get to see her or talk to her again.

"Earth to Bas!"

I blinked when Charlotte stood in front of me and waved her hand in my face.

"You totally spaced out on me just then," she said, grinning at me.

"Sorry about that," I said. "Let's head back downstairs."

"What's her name?"

"Who?" I asked, feigning ignorance about what she was talking about.

"The girl who has you all in la-la land," Charlotte teased.

I sighed and shoved my hands in my pockets as we headed for the back of the bookstore. There was no use in keeping it from her. She would hound me until I gave up the information she wanted.

"Carmen," I said, as we reached the secret bookshelf door.

"Pretty name," Charlotte said. "Is she pretty?"

"Gorgeous."

"How long have you two been dating?"

"We've gone out a couple of times over the last few weeks."

"Will I get to meet her?"

"The jury's still out on that one. Ouch!" I rubbed my arm where she socked me really hard.

"Why can't I meet her?" she whined.

"I told you, we've only gone out a couple of times. I don't want to freak her out by introducing her to you too soon."

"I'm only in town for a couple of days, Bas."

"Maybe," I acquiesced. "If you promise not to go all 'crazy big sister' on her."

I pulled the false book to unlock the door and pulled it open.

"Age before beauty," I teased, encouraging her to head down the stairs first, earning me an eye-roll.

I closed the door behind me and followed Charlotte down the stairs. Since it was the middle of the day, the club was closed. It was only opened for special events Monday through Wednesday nights.

"You'll have to come back tomorrow night to see the place when it's truly alive," I said, unlocking the door and opening it.

"Bas!" Charlotte gushed. "It looks great down here. I'm definitely going to come back."

She looked around and then turned to face me.

"Where's Reilly?" she asked.

"He's on his way back from England," I said. "He went to visit his parents."

"Speaking of visiting parents..."

Damn, I'd walked right into that one.

"I'm going to see Mom and Dad before we fly back to California." She was gentle as she asked, "When's the last time you saw them, Bas?"

"I talk to Mom fairly often."

"That's not what I asked you, Sebastian. When's the last time you *saw* them? As in went for a visit?"

My parents were about a five-hour drive away from where I lived. Admittedly, I didn't visit them as often as I used to. But there was one large, unsettling reason for that.

"Thanksgiving," I said, turning away from her.

"Oh, that's not so bad."

"The last Thanksgiving you were there," I added. Charlotte hadn't come home last year because she and Gabe had decided to spend Thanksgiving with his family.

"Sebastian!" Charlotte said, shocked. "That was nearly *two years* ago."

"I know how long it's been, Char," I said, growing agitated with the direction the conversation was going.

"You and Dad can't *possibly* still be on the outs about all of this."

"You would think?" I mumbled.

"Have you reached out to him?"

"Have *I*–" I whirled around to face her. "Do you know every time I call Mom and ask to speak to him, he refuses to talk to me? She covers for him, making up some kind of excuse of him not being able to come to the phone, but I know the truth. Did you know that he hasn't even come to visit the bookstore since it opened? And we've been open for over a year."

"Well, this is *my* first time here so–"

"It's not the same, Char," I said, shaking my head, trying to keep the hurt out of my voice. "You live across the country, you have a career, and a family. Besides that, Mom came for the grand opening. Dad just didn't come with her."

"Are you serious?" Charlotte asked quietly.

I nodded, hating to talk about this.

It had been during Thanksgiving that I announced that I was leaving my career in teaching to open a bookstore. My dad, who'd been a teacher for over thirty years, had gone ballistic. Of course, he railed at my decision, saying I was throwing away all the years of schooling I'd gone through.

I'd tried to explain to him that teaching just wasn't my passion, but he'd shut me down and shut me out. We hadn't spoken since then, despite my best efforts.

"You need to go and talk to him," Charlotte insisted. "Face to face."

"Why should I spare the effort when he hasn't given me the same courtesy?" I said through clenched teeth.

Charlotte threw her hands in the air. "Both of you are stubborn as all get out. Where do you think *you* get it from?"

I shook my head, now in need of a drink.

"Whatever," I said, heading for the door. "Can we *please* talk about something else?"

"Fine," she relented. Then she smiled and said, "Tell me more about this Carmen."

CHAPTER TWELVE

"**W**ill you chill?"

I smiled, as I looked over at Heather, who was fidgeting in the seat next to me in the back the of cab that was taking us to 154.

Heather looked amazing in her outfit, though she seemed ridiculously uncomfortable; and I was dressed to impress one Sebastian Kincaid in my black bodycon dress, with sheer mesh inserts around the waist and up one side of the skirt, that gave an extra little peek at my midriff, as well as one of my thighs. It was definitely a sans-underwear dress.

I'd had to drag Heather out with me tonight giving her a long overdue Mom's Night Out, something she didn't do nearly enough. We were also celebrating the fact that Heather had put in her two weeks' notice at Mason and Dunn. By the time I got back from my trip to L.A., she'd officially be my executive assistant again.

I watched as Heather reached into her purse and pulled out her phone.

"What are you doing?" I asked, watching her fingers fly across her phone's screen.

"I'm texting my mom to see...hey!" she cried out after I snatched her phone away.

"Your mama said not to be texting her every five minutes about Tevin. Let her enjoy her 'nana time' with that boy. And you need to relax and enjoy your kid-free time."

We pulled in front of the bookstore right then. Heather looked at me, expecting me to hand over her phone, but instead, I shoved it into my own purse and then paid the taxi driver. We climbed out of the car and went into the bookstore.

I waved at Suzette who was working the bar and she winked and nodded at me, giving me the okay to head to the false bookshelf. Apparently I'd earned a VIP status of sorts, thanks to my relationship with Sebastian.

When we got to the back, I found the book to unlock the door and pulled it, grinning as I looked over my shoulder at Heather, who seemed to be intrigued with what I was doing.

"This is something else," Heather said, as we went down the stairs.

"Why are you whispering?" I giggled.

"I don't know," she said. "It's just so cryptic."

I understood the allure as we finally reached the door where the same bouncer, who'd been there the first time I visited, was dutifully keeping guard. He nodded stiffly, and reached behind him to open the door that would allow us into the club.

"Wow," Heather said, looking around.

"I know, right?"

We headed to the bar, where we both ordered drinks and then sat back and relaxed, enjoying the music.

"You know," Heather said, after taking a sip of her tropical martini, "This place would be great for Bobby's book launch party."

"You're right," I agreed. "I'll run it by Sebastian soon."

"Where is he anyway?" Heather asked, searching the room.

"Probably working," I said with a shrug.

I'd briefly mentioned to Sebastian the last time we talked that Heather and I would be swinging through, but I knew he was working tonight, so I didn't expect him to drop everything for me once we arrived.

I saw him a moment later, working his way through the crowded club. My grip tightened around my glass as I watched a woman attempt to brush up against him flirtatiously. I felt a sense of relief when he shook his head, smiled and, as politely as he could, backed out of her reach.

"Could you *be* more jealous?" Heather snickered.

"Shut up," I snapped before taking a long sip of my drink.

Okay, yes, I may have been jealous for a millisecond. But the way Sebastian had responded to the woman's advances quickly put my mind at ease. I'm sure it would have been easy for a man in his position – a young, *gorgeous*, black business owner – to take advantage of his status and all the...perks that it afforded him. But he seemed genuinely disinterested. I could only hope that a part of the reason for that was me.

He seemed to validate my hope by the smile on his face when he turned and saw me at the bar.

He weaved his way through the crowd, straight toward

me and I hopped off of my barstool to stand and greet him, making sure he got an eyeful of my dress.

"Good evening ladies," he said, even though he was looking directly at me. He leaned forward and kissed me on the cheek and then turned to Heather and held out a hand.

"Sebastian Kincaid," he said, giving her a warm smile.

"Heather Braggs," she said, shaking his hand. "Nice to finally meet you."

"Likewise," he said, and then turned to face me again.

"You've got a full house tonight," I said.

"We do," Sebastian said nodding. "I wish I could be a better host tonight, but–"

I held up my hand to cut him off. "We can handle ourselves," I said, with a wink.

Sebastian nodded, pulling his lip between his teeth as his eyes raked over my body.

"Well at the very least, I can seat you ladies." He turned and held his arm out to Heather and she looped her arm through his. Instead of offering me his other arm, he took my hand into his, interlocking our fingers, before leading the way back through the crowd.

We happened to pass the table belonging to the woman who'd attempted – and failed – to push up on Sebastian a few minutes earlier. She gave me the evilest eye, and I returned it with a satisfied smirk on my lips and an extra swish in my hips.

Sebastian took us to a table that had a reserved sign on top of it. He removed the sign and waved his hand over the table with a small flourish.

"Ladies," he said, holding out the chairs for us, first Heather and then me.

I shivered when I felt Sebastian discreetly run his fingers up my side, before brushing a kiss against my neck.

"It looks like you two could use refills," he said after he stood back up. "I'll go and put those orders in for you."

We nodded and watched as he disappeared in the crowd again.

"Girl!" Heather swooned. "He's so...*oomph*."

I laughed at Heather's reaction to Sebastian. "I agree. He is pretty oomph-worthy."

"And so is *he*," she uttered, clutching my arm. I followed her line of vision and smiled at the familiar face.

"That's Reilly," I said. "Sebastian's best friend and business partner."

I held up my hand and waved, and Heather's nails dug deeper into my arm. "What are you doing?" she asked.

"I'm getting his attention so I can say hello and introduce you," I said, continuing to wave until he saw us. He smiled and strolled towards us as I peeled Heather's fingers out of my forearm.

"Welcome back," I said when Reilly made it to the table.

"Good to see you again, love," he said. He turned to Heather, looking rather intrigued. "Who is your friend?"

"Reilly Lawrence, this is my best friend, Heather Braggs."

I watched as Reilly greeted Heather much like the way he'd greeted me when we first met. But their interaction was...different. When their eyes connected, there was an obvious connection, and Reilly's lips lingered on the back of Heather's hand for a tad bit longer than when he'd kissed my hand just to get under Sebastian's skin.

"You ladies enjoy the rest of your evening," Reilly said, finally breaking his eye contact with Heather. The waiter arrived with our drinks and Reilly took them and set them down in front of us. "And if you need anything, don't hesitate to ask."

Once Reilly was gone, I turned to Heather, smiling at her.

"You two seemed to hit it off rather nicely," I said.

"Hmph, pass," she said before bringing her glass to her lips.

I stared at Heather dumbfounded. "I'm sorry – *what*?"

"He's not what I'm looking for," she said.

"What you're looking for? You two were practically tearing each other's clothes off with your eyes and he's...not what you're looking for?"

Heather looked around and lowered her voice.

"You *know* what my plans are," she said. "Sure, the chemistry was great just now. But how long do you think that would last? Furthermore, do you *actually* think a guy like that has any plans of settling down any time soon?"

I could have argued with her that she never knew what could happen, but Heather's biological clock seemed to be ticking at maximum speed and she wasn't letting anything distract her from her ultimate goal of having another baby.

Not even the handsome British man who couldn't seem to stop looking our way the rest of the night.

"I will say this," Heather said dreamily. "He would make some exquisite babies."

We spent the rest of the evening enjoying the live music, food and drinks. Both Sebastian and Reilly came back by our table several times to check on us. Sebastian even introduced me to his sister, who was visiting from out of town. She seemed sweet, but didn't stay long.

When we asked for the check at the end of the night, the waiter informed us that there was no check. I made sure to leave a hefty tip and then we left out of the door that took us directly outside, since the bookstore was closed for the night.

My phone vibrated in my purse and when I reached for it, I noticed Heather's phone as well. I handed it back to her with a smile and then pulled out mine.

My heart skipped a beat or two when I saw the text from Sebastian.

Sebastian: I'm going to be thinking of you in that dress all night now.

That was the intention, I teased in my response.

He sent an emoji of a face in pain and I stifled a laugh.

Sebastian: Our next date is this weekend.

I know.

Sebastian: Don't forget, when I take you back to your place after the opera, I'm coming inside...for more than coffee.

I nibbled on my lip, turned on by his subtle reminder of what was in store for us. I thought about how to reply and decided to go with the straightforward approach.

I can't wait...

CHAPTER THIRTEEN

Sebastian

I stood at Carmen's door waiting for her to answer after I'd rang the doorbell. When she finally answered, my heart actually began to race at the sight of her.

"Are you ready for some opera?" she said with a teasing grin on her face.

I rolled my eyes and made a snoring sound and she giggled.

"Oh, it won't be *that* bad."

"I'm just messing with you," I chuckled. "I actually am looking forward to it."

I wasn't ashamed to admit that a large part of the reason was because it meant I got to spend time with her again. I'd do just about anything, if it meant spending more time with her.

"Plus, I have to report back to Rye, he's really into this type of stuff," I added as my eyes roved over her body.

As usual, she looked amazing and it made me want to reach out and touch her.

So, I did.

I pulled her into my arms and roamed my hands up and down her body.

"You sure we can't catch another showing?" I tempted, as I lowered my head, brushing my nose against her neck. She smelled so sweet that I found myself running my tongue along the side of her neck.

I thought about her text a few nights ago.

I can't wait...

I couldn't either, and now that I had her in my arms in her apartment, it was hard to think of anything besides what it would feel like to finally slide deep inside of her.

She let out a sexy little laugh, running her hands up my chest before grabbing hold of the lapels of my suit jacket.

"It's opening night," she said. "So, no, we can't."

I nodded, and then took her chin between my fingers, careful not to mess up her makeup.

"I suppose this will have to suffice," I said, before lightly pressing my lips to hers. I felt her fingers tighten around my jacket lapels as I deepened the kiss, while my hands moved down to cup her firm ass.

Carmen was the first to pull away. She blew out a ragged breath and shook her head.

"We can't be late," she chastised weakly, as she reached up and wiped her lipstick from my mouth. She looked in the mirror by the door, reached into her purse, pulling out her lipstick. Once she reapplied the lipstick that I'd thoroughly kissed off, she was ready to go.

I was already thinking of how things would play out once we returned to her place.

I glanced over at Carmen when I heard her sniffling. I

reached into the inside pocket of my suit jacket and pulled out my handkerchief and slid it into her hand. I felt her squeeze my hand in thanks, and my hand went to gently pat her thigh in consolation.

So, comfort may have only been *part* of my motive in reaching over to touch her bare skin, but I couldn't help myself. From the moment she'd opened her door, standing in front of me in that body hugging, floor length dress that had not one, but two damn near obscene splits up the front, my mind – and body – had been in overdrive.

The only reason I hadn't tried harder to convince her to skip the opera was because her friend was headlining the production and as she'd mentioned at her apartment, it was opening night.

I had to admit, even though *everything* about Carmen was a distraction, the opera was pretty damn dope. It was captivating and I understood why Carmen was so moved by it that she'd actually shed a few tears.

I went to remove my hand from Carmen's thigh. I figured I'd indulged long enough. I was surprised when she covered my hand with hers, keeping it in place.

I raised a captivated brow as my eyes drifted back over to Carmen. She softly cleared her throat and shifted in her seat, sitting up a bit straighter and my hand ended up deeper between her legs.

Since she was welcoming my touch, I decided to explore a little further. Thanks to Carmen's connection to one of the stars of the show, we had box seats and we were the only two in the box. Her breath hitched, and my eyes fell to the sudden rise and fall of her breasts and my fingers dug into the supple skin of her inner thigh.

Her eyes drifted closed and she let out the sexiest little whimper, biting her lip to keep quiet. My dick strained against my slacks when she opened her legs a bit more, inviting my hand to journey higher. My fingers grazed the crotch of her damp thong, her arousal filled my nostrils and my mouth began to water.

I swear, I must have been a man possessed or something. This woman had me feeling so fucking horny, that I didn't think about my next moves. All I knew in that moment was that if I didn't taste her, I might actually lose my mind.

I 'accidentally' dropped my binoculars and they ended up under my seat, requiring me to crouch down on the floor out of sight. I looked up to find Carmen's curious and heated gaze on me.

I gave her a hot grin, before reaching up to flick the flap of the front of her dress over one of her thighs, even more thankful that she'd chosen to wear a dress with two splits.

I showed her just how thankful I was when I pulled her thong to the side and buried my head between her legs.

Sweet mercy!

I was getting *way* more than I'd bargained for when I decided to boldly keep Sebastian's hand on my leg.

Now, he was on his knees, pressing *my* knees wide open while I tried to keep my composure and not draw attention to our balcony. I wriggled at the nibbling of his lips on one thigh and then the other.

I sucked in a deep breath when he slid my thong to the side and the tip of his tongue swiped against my clit. My stomach clenched and I gripped the handles of my chair when he licked me in long, languid strokes. He took his time, as if we had all the time in the world, as if he was doing this to me in a bedroom, rather than a fucking balcony at the opera.

But I didn't give a damn where we were at that moment, just as long as he–

"Don't stop," I whispered harshly. "Oh god, don't stop."

He chuckled quietly and I felt the vibrations rumble against me, or maybe they were the vibrations *inside* of me from the orgasm building up. I couldn't tell the difference. And I didn't care.

The music and the female performer began to crescendo at the same time as my orgasm did. I let out a strangled cry. I couldn't help it. Sebastian had given me an out of this world release with just his mouth. I sat there trying to get my breathing regulated, while he delicately fixed my underwear and put the front of my dress back in place.

I then watched him as he stood, fixed his jacket and grinned at me wickedly as he said, "If you'll excuse me. I need to make a quick trip to the men's room."

He returned several minutes later and sat back down next to me and picked up his binoculars. He sat there watching the performance as if he hadn't been eating me out like I was the best damn dessert he'd ever had not even twenty minutes ago.

He smelled of fresh soap, so I knew he'd washed my scent from him.

One would have thought that after what he'd done to me, I'd be relaxed and calm.

But I was anything but those things.

If anything, I was even more aroused, even more eager to get out of here and back to my place.

He'd given me one hell of a preview of what I could look forward to later tonight. Honestly, if I hadn't promised Donnie that we'd go backstage afterwards to see him, I would have told Sebastian I was ready to go. Right. Now.

The pulsing between my thighs increased more and more every time I remembered the sight of his head between my legs, his hands sliding under me to palm my ass. Every inch of my skin now felt hypersensitive – hyper-aware of Sebastian's nearness.

I was beyond ready for him to make love to me, and if it didn't happen soon...

It *had* to happen soon.

Finally, the opera came to its conclusion and we stood.

"I need to stop by the restroom," I said quietly, and Sebastian nodded.

I hurried into the restroom, thankful that it wasn't crowded, thanks to it being in a more private section, and freshened up.

I looked in the mirror, surprised by how flushed I looked. I pulled out my compact and added a little powder to my face for a touch up, and hoping to hide the evidence that I'd had absolutely naughty things done to me in those box seats earlier.

When I considered myself sufficiently calmed down, I left the bathroom.

Sebastian was waiting for me, standing propped against the wall, looking cool and collected, while I stood there staring at him.

I was ready to climb all over him.

He pushed off the wall and came over to me.

"You said you promised your friend we'd go back and see him, right?" he asked, looking down at me.

All I could do was nod.

He took my hand in his and his lip quirked up. "Well then let's go. The sooner we speak to your friend, the sooner we can get out of here."

I nodded again, recognizing his unspoken words.

Donatello was thrilled to see me backstage. I introduced him to Sebastian and they hit it off well.

I stood there in awe, watching as Sebastian discussed the show as if he hadn't spent a portion of it...preoccupied. I was already planning on coming back to see it again. Probably alone so I wouldn't be distracted.

Donnie drank in Sebastian's praise and he gave me a subtle nod of approval.

"Go!" he said eventually. "Go and enjoy the rest of your night. It is still very young, yes?"

"Yes," I said, as I hugged him.

Donatello turned and gave Sebastian one last handshake.

"One evening, when you are visiting my Carmen, you will come by for dinner?" he asked.

"I'd be honored," Sebastian said.

We left the performance hall; the ride back to my place was filled with a heady silence.

My fingers trembled with anticipation as I unlocked my door.

Sebastian's large body surrounded me from behind, his hand looping around my waist.

When I finally managed to get the door opened, I

turned to ask the question that I already knew the answer to.

I didn't even get a chance to get the words out before his mouth was on mine and we were tumbling into my apartment.

CHAPTER FOURTEEN

"I s it safe to assume you don't want coffee?" I managed to tease as I released a trembling breath at the feel of Sebastian's lips on my neck.

"Maybe in the morning," he rasped. "Right now, the only thing I want is this dress off you."

His mouth came down on mine again, searing my lips with another kiss. I gently tugged his neck as I haphazardly walked backwards, heading to the bedroom. I shoved his jacket off as he undid his tie and then my fingers furiously began unbuttoning his dress shirt.

We finally made it to my room as he unzipped my dress. He slowly – *so* slowly – pulled it down. I shrugged out of the top of the dress and the rest fell to my feet leaving me standing in my black lace bra, matching thong and heels.

Sebastian just stood there drinking me in. My nipples hardened, the tingling between my legs intensified.

My pulse raced when his fingers reached out and skated across my collarbone before moving down to cover one of my breasts. My nipples grew even more rigid beneath his palm.

"I want you so damn bad, Carmen," he said into my ear, his teeth gently scraping the underside of my jaw.

My hands went to his slacks and I undid the belt followed by the button and zipper. My breathing grew heavy as he kicked off his shoes and socks and pushed down his pants. I drank him in, from his broad shoulders and sinewy biceps down to his powerful thighs that were slightly bowed. Everything about Sebastian Kincaid was arousing.

He grabbed me by my hip and yanked me against his hard body, his mouth covering mines. We sank down into the bed, and I relished in the feeling of him on top of me. Our hands seemed to be everywhere as we explored each other's body.

When his hand slid beneath my panties, his fingers dipped into my folds, my hips bucked on their own accord.

"Bas," I moaned.

"You tasted so sweet," he murmured into my ear, reminding me of what he'd done to me earlier tonight at the opera.

"I want you inside of me," I nearly begged.

I was beyond ready to feel him inside of me. We'd basically been dancing around our sexual attraction since the day we'd met. We both seemed to have known that this exact moment had been inescapable.

His fingers moved faster and faster inside of me and suddenly they were gone, leaving my body humming. He pulled away and reached down to pick his pants up from the floor. He quickly found his wallet and pulled out a condom.

In no time, he was covered and he'd sat back on his haunches, gazing down at me with an intensity I'd never seen in his eyes before.

"Open for me," he commanded.

In that moment, I thought of the spoken word poem he'd performed on our first date at his club.

It made me even wetter.

I spread my legs wide and he reached down, slowly removing my underwear. He did everything at such an unhurried pace. I was squirming on the bed; nearly desperate by the time he tossed my panties out of the way and grabbed my hips, propping them up.

But oh...

It was *so* worth the wait when he finally slid inside of me – nice and slowly, of course.

He swore under his breath, gripping my hips as he pulled out of me and then sank back in over and over again.

He came back down over me, making us chest to chest and he buried his face into my neck. My nails dug into his shoulders as my body coiled.

He sensed it. He was so attuned to my body; it was...out of this world.

"Sebastian!" I cried out, squeezing my eyes shut.

I felt his lips on mine right when I came apart in his arms.

He didn't stop. In fact, his movements sped up. I felt his muscles bunch and he let out a ragged groan as he went over the edge.

I woke up to the smell of food wafting into my bedroom. I sat up, pushed my hair out of my face and squinted as I looked around. I shifted in the bed and when I felt that delicious soreness between my legs, memories from last night came rushing back.

Sebastian.

The things we'd done.

We'd gone at it a couple more times after that first time, each better than the last.

The way he touched me, the way he moved against me – *inside* of me. The incredibly nasty things he whispered in my ear, as we got lost in our passion; the things *I'd* said!

One night with him and I was hooked. It was almost shameful.

But I wasn't ashamed, not one bit.

I was somehow *still* horny. And hungry, judging by the way my stomach growled.

I pushed the blanket from over my naked body, and swung my feet over the edge of the bed. I padded over to my dresser and pulled out an extra-large T-shirt and shrugged into it.

Sebastian was obviously still there since the enticing aroma of food had me floating through the condo feeling like a damn cartoon character. But he had to have left because–

"You sure are a hard person to cook for, Bun. Your cupboards are literally bare."

His back was to me as I entered the kitchen, but he'd obviously heard my approach.

I angled my head to the side and with a confused look on my face asked, "Bun?"

I watched as he nodded his head. "Came up with it last night, after we left the opera."

That damn opera.

He finally looked over his shoulder, his eyes sweeping from my toes up to my eyes. "That's my nickname for you now."

"Whyyyy?" I asked, still confused.

"'Cause your pussy is crazy sweet, like one of those good ass cinnamon buns."

My mouth fell open, my cheeks flushed and he chuckled, turning back to focus on whatever he was whipping up at the stove. I wanted to call him corny for coming up with that nickname. Any other man who'd called me some kind of term of endearment relating to food would have gotten an earful. But when Sebastian called me Bun...My insides turned all gooey.

"You let me go down on you at the opera and *now* you wanna act shy?" He continued chuckling. "Get over here, Bun. Breakfast is ready."

I slid onto one of the bar stools at the island as he pushed a plate of steaming hot French toast and fresh fruit in front of me.

"Coffee," he said with a wink, as he placed a steaming cup next to my plate. I smiled when I noticed that he'd used my favorite mug.

I surveyed the display of food in front of me. It looked freaking amazing and I was eager to dig in.

"So, he cooks too?" I said, finally finding my voice again.

Sebastian grinned as he sat down in the seat next to me and we began to eat.

The food was...heavenly.

I forked another piece of the French toast that was drizzled in maple syrup and powdered sugar and shoved it in my mouth, rolling my eyes and moaning.

"It's sounds like that, that's got a brother rushin' out to the store to buy stuff to make this breakfast for you," he mumbled, before popping a strawberry into his mouth.

I smiled and shook my head.

"I'm not much of a cook," I admitted before taking a sip of my coffee, which was also perfect. "I've been eating out a lot lately since I've been busy with the upswing in my business, so I haven't really taken the time to grocery shop. That and..."

I stopped talking before I embarrassed myself.

But Sebastian finished my sentence for me.

"And your money was tight?"

I glanced over at him and our eyes met.

"I found some noodles when I was searching for something to cook," he said, like it was no big deal.

So I tried to go for aloof as I said, "Did you ever consider that I just like eating them 'cause they're quick and foolproof?"

He shrugged as he cut another piece of French toast. "That may be the case, but I remember you saying that you'd had a rough year when we first met."

I looked away, but he grabbed my chin and forced me to look at him. "Hey, it's nothing to be ashamed of, Bun."

"I'm *not* ashamed," I snapped. My eyes fell closed and I blew out a breath. "I'm sorry. I'm just...not used to really talking about this with anyone." No one *really* knew just how bad things had gotten for me. Hell, I still hadn't even told my father about it.

Sebastian nodded and released my chin, leaning forward to plant a kiss on my lips.

"I understand that," he said, turning back to his food. "But you're straight now, right? With your funds?"

His concern was...endearing.

"Of course," I said. "Like I said, I just haven't had the time to go and get groceries. Plus, Donnie makes sure I'm fed."

"Good. If you ever need anything just let me know."

I immediately began to shake my head.

"Bas, you don't have to–"

"If you ever need anything, *let me know*, Bun," he repeated, leaving no room for argument.

I certainly hadn't expected anything like this the morning after an amazing night, but it felt good. With Sebastian, I felt...safe. He made it easy to confide in him. And when he looked at me when we discussed my previous hardships, he didn't look at me with pity, but with understanding.

So instead of trying to act all hard like 'Cut-Throat Carmen', the independent, bad chick who could do it all with no one's help, I simply replied with a grateful, "Okay."

It was nice to know that even though I didn't feel like I *needed* anyone's help, the offer from Sebastian was there.

CHAPTER FIFTEEN

Sebastian

I strolled into By the Books late and with a grin on my face that I couldn't get rid of no matter how hard I tried. Since it was Monday, I tipped my head to Suzette, who was getting her barista on, and headed straight for my office.

I booted up my desktop, dropped down in my chair, and pulled out my phone. I smiled at the text Carmen sent me.

Carmen.

That woman was something else. After we finished breakfast, she dragged me back to the room, where we spent the rest of the morning and most of the afternoon.

She reminded me of how she'd earned the nickname 'Bun'.

I was thoroughly satisfied in how–

"You finally got shagged!"

My head popped up to find Reilly standing in the doorway grinning at me like a loon.

"Can you at least come in and shut the fucking door? I'd rather not have all my business out on display," I murmured, returning my focus back to responding to Carmen, who wanted to know if I could come back after work.

My Bun was insatiable.

My fingers paused in their typing as that thought flew across my mind. Was I really calling her *my* Bun?

You gave her that corny ass nickname, may as well, my thoughts rang out.

Flashes of the way she'd come undone over and over under me – and on top of me – filled my mind. The way those stormy grey eyes of hers went wild, widening with dilation, and then rolling back as she moaned.

Hell yeah, she was my Bun.

"So?"

I lifted my eyes up to Reilly, realizing that he'd closed the door and had sat down in the chair across from me, lifting his leg to plant it on my desk. I slapped it back down before it made contact.

"You're worse than these gossiping ass females that come in here, you know?" I said, finishing my text. I set my phone down and gave my friend my undivided attention. "What do you want to know?"

"How was it?"

I rolled my eyes.

"I mean...it was..."

Amazing, spectacular...so good it had me running out to buy food to make her breakfast the next morning. I don't recall ever making a woman breakfast after sex.

I shrugged, shooting for low key. But Rye saw right through my bullshit.

He threw his head back and let out the loudest chortle.

"Aye, mate. She got you all wound up in the britches, eh? Musta been top notch quality!"

I shook my head.

"We went to the opera, which was great by the way."

Though I wasn't referring to the show. "Then we went back to her place. We had a good time."

I decided not to go into detail about exactly what happened at the opera between me and Carmen. Some things were better left between the parties involved. It kept them more memorable.

Reilly stood.

"I'm happy for ya, truly. Maybe now you won't be all uptight, like your pops seems to have been late–"

I looked up again as Reilly's eyes shifted around the room uncomfortably.

"My pops?" I said. "You've been in contact with my pops?"

Reilly's hand went to the back of his neck. "Technically, we've never been *out* of contact."

Un-fucking-believable.

My parents had known Reilly since our college days at Oxford. They loved him, considered him their 'British son'. So it shouldn't have surprised me that my father and Rye were still in touch, yet...

I rocked back and forth in my chair, trying to keep whatever emotions that were beginning to roll through me in check.

"When's the last time you talked to him?" I demanded.

Reilly blew out a breath. "Couple of days ago."

That shit stung more than I expected it to.

"So, he's cool with *you* giving up your career on Wall Street to pursue your dreams, but he's still feeling some kind of way about me doing the exact same thing?" I nodded. "Great."

"I'm not his son, so it's not the same," Reilly said, earning him a look that clearly asked *whose side are you on?*

Though I didn't voice that question out loud, Reilly still answered it. "I'm on your side, mate. I'm just stating facts here. And don't think for a second I don't catch hell every time I go home to visit my parents. But at least I'm goin' home."

"Yo, what the hell is that supposed to me?" I growled.

"You know exactly what it means, Bas. No need for me to spell it out for you."

I shook my head. "I've got work to do, man," I said, effectively shutting down this conversation.

"Right," Reilly said, turning to open the door to leave. He paused and looked over his shoulder. "You need to go see him, Sebastian," he insisted and then left.

I typed in the passcode on my computer and got lost in my work.

I didn't want to think about my father and how I'd obviously been a complete disappointment to him.

That shit fucked up my head every time I dwelled on it for too long.

Carmen

"I've got a favor to ask."

Sebastian, who'd been eerily quiet, looked up and smiled.

"Name it."

We were out having lunch at a Pho restaurant. I pushed my noodles around with my chopsticks and looked up at him.

He hadn't even heard my request, yet he was primed to say yes. It reminded me of the conversation we'd had over breakfast when he said if I ever needed anything to let him know.

"We're gearing up for the release of Bobby's launch. It should be in a few months."

Sebastian nodded. "That's great."

My lips tilted up. "Yeah. Heather mentioned that 154 would be a great place to have it. So, I was wondering if it would be possible to rent the place out?"

"You know I got you and Bobby, Bun," Sebastian said, bringing his chopsticks up to his mouth. "Just shoot me the details; the date, expected number of people, all of that and I'll take care of it."

My smile widened. "Great. And make sure to send me a quote."

Sebastian shook his head as he finished the food in his mouth. "No charge, Bun."

"Bas–"

"No charge. Bobby is my boy. Been coming to By the Books since we opened. He's a loyal customer." He paused, and then said, "Scratch that. He's *family*. So, hosting the party for the launching of his book would be an honor. No charge."

"Are you doing this because we're sleeping together?"

I'd asked him for this as a favor, yes. But I was still looking at it from a business perspective.

Sebastian rolled his eyes and looked at me. "Carmen, I'd probably insist that Bobby have the launch party at my spot even if I'd never met you. So no, it's not because we're sleeping together."

I sighed and looked away. "I'm sorry."

"It's all good, Bun," he said, grinning at me. "You can make it up to me later tonight."

This time, I rolled my eyes.

"You ready to get out of here?"

"Yes," I said, pushing out of my chair.

Sebastian paid for lunch and we headed for the door.

"I'm taking you to the airport this weekend, right?"

My trip to the writers' conference in L.A. was coming up.

I opened my mouth to confirm our plans when the door swung open and I froze.

Shit!

I should have known better than to come to *this* restaurant. It wasn't that far from Mason and Dunn.

I stood face to face – for the first time in over a year – with Lee.

His eyes took me in from head to toe before smiling.

"Car-Car–" I *hated* that name. "Been a long time."

I was seething. But I couldn't move. I couldn't speak. I'd always wondered what I'd say if and when I ever saw Lee again. I always expected to eloquently tell him off from top to bottom, and tell him exactly where he could go.

But now that my moment had finally arrived, I stood there rigid, unable to form a sentence.

"Aye Bun, you good, baby?"

Sebastian's voice seemed to bring me out of my stupor.

"Yes, let's go," I said.

Lee, however, apparently wasn't ready to let us pass just yet.

He had the nerve to try and size Bas up. Then he took a step forward and held a hand out to Sebastian.

"Lee Graham, an old friend of Carmen's."

Sebastian's lip quirked up coolly as he reached out to shake Lee's hand. I heard Lee grunt as Sebastian squeezed his hand tighter than what was probably considered polite and something inside of me was amused by that.

"Sebastian Kincaid," he said, and then he slid his free hand around my waist protectively. "A *new* friend of Carmen's."

They released hands and Lee discreetly balled up his hand and then released it.

He turned his attention back to me.

"Car-Car. Good to see you again."

I shook my head, disgusted by the sight of Lee and grabbed Sebastian's hand, practically dragging him out of the restaurant.

"Ex-boyfriend?" Sebastian asked curiously once we'd walked a good distance down the sidewalk.

"The *worst*," I grumbled.

"He didn't put his hands on you or anything like that, did he?"

I looked up, surprised by the irate look in his eyes. I didn't have a doubt that Sebastian would go back and knock Lee on his ass.

"No," I said, shaking my head. "He was just a real asshole. I ignored the signs until it was over."

I was still frustrated with myself, especially when I remembered that bum ass breakup email he'd sent. He had the *nerve* to look at me today as if everything was just sunshine and flowers. Why couldn't I have said *something*? Anything! I couldn't even form a decent 'go fuck yourself'.

But Sebastian seemed to have sensed my discomfort in Lee's presence and stepped up.

"You okay?" Sebastian asked.

Thanks to him coming to my aid.

"Yeah," I said, feeling more and more at ease the further we were from the restaurant. "I'm okay."

But I'd have to find a new Pho restaurant.

That kinda made me sad.

CHAPTER SIXTEEN

Sebastian

We arrived at the airport and after parking, I pulled her bag out of my trunk and walked her inside. We'd both been quiet on the drive to the airport. I couldn't quite gauge what may have been on her mind, but I was too busy in my own head.

I'd come to the startling realization that I was going to miss this woman.

"This is where we part ways," I said, setting her bag down in front of her.

Carmen nodded and looked away for a moment. Her eyes looked slightly glossy and then she blinked several times before she smiled up at me.

"Don't forget about me while I'm gone, Kincaid," she teased.

She was only going to be gone for a week, but already it felt like it would be longer.

"You know that's not going to happen, Bun," I said, pulling her into my arms.

She rose on her toes and palmed my face between her

hands and gave me the sweetest kiss. I tightened my grip around her waist when her tongue slid into my mouth. I pulled away when I felt my dick begin to stir. The last thing I wanted was to walk out of here sporting a massive hard-on.

"Call me when you make it to L.A.," I said.

"I will."

She pulled up the handle on her rolling luggage and gave me one last kiss before turning to head for security.

I stood there, with my hands in my pockets, watching her walk away. The sway of her hips was so enticing.

I shook my head as I turned to leave the airport.

Damn I couldn't wait until her ass got back.

Carmen

"This is really good."

I looked up at the writer sitting across the table from me in the hotel lounge.

"Really?" she asked, nervously wringing her hands together.

I nodded, taking a sip of my drink.

I hadn't seen her at the conference, but I knew she'd attended from the laminated lanyard she had hanging around her neck that was like mine.

It was the last day of the conference and I'd networked my ass off. I'd met with some writers that had the potential to one day turn into clients of mine and I'd also met with other agents. I was surprised when some of them handed me their card, offering their services if I was ever in the market to create a team.

I tucked those away, because as Heather had previously mentioned, I just may need to hire more agents one day.

I held up the bound papers and asked, "Do you mind if I keep these?"

The woman's eyes rounded.

"Really?"

That seemed to be the only word she knew now.

"Yes," I said, giving her a smile. "I'd like to read over it some more. If I feel like you're a good fit for my business you can expect a call within thirty to sixty days."

"Oh, my gosh," she breathed. "Thank you so much!"

We chatted for a few more minutes and then she took off.

I finished my drink and looked down at the copy of the first three chapters of the manuscript the woman had left with me. I already knew I'd offer my services to her. I could usually tell within the first chapter if the writer had what it took.

This woman – an African-American contemporary romance author – was crazy talented. We needed more authors like her telling tales of black love. And I was going to help get her stories out there to the world.

The waiter came by and asked if I wanted another drink and I said yes. Since I didn't have to get up early in the morning, I was indulging. I sat back in my chair and pulled out my phone, smiling when I saw a text from Sebastian.

Sebastian: Starving for my Bun.

You can have as much of your Bun as you want when I get back, I replied.

Sebastian: Counting down the days.

Me too.

"Texting your '*new* friend'?"

The grip on my phone tightened and I blew out an irritated breath through my nose.

While the conference had been relatively great, there was one blaring blemish – Lee.

I was surprised to see him here. When we were dating, and worked together, he wouldn't have been caught dead at a writers' conference. He thought he was above 'panhandling for clients' as he so asshole-ishly put it. So it never even crossed my mind that he'd be here. Yet, much to my chagrin, here he was.

I'd managed to avoid him the entire time, until now.

My first inclination was to just ignore him and hope he'd get the hint to leave me alone. But, of course, he wasn't going to do that.

"I looked him up," Lee said, pulling out a chair, inviting himself to sit down. "Sebastian Kincaid. Teacher turned bookstore owner. Quite the downgrade, Car-Car."

That had me seeing red.

This barely-graduated-from-community college ass bastard had some nerve.

"First of all," I spat out as I slammed my phone down. "You have *zero* right to go snooping around on the man I'm involved with. You have no kind of claim on me."

"So you're just gonna throw away everything we had?" he asked. "For some...glorified librarian ass dude."

"Throw everything away? You're talking like there was actually a chance of ever getting back together; which there *definitely* is not. And I'm sorry, but I think you're confused on who threw everything away, Lee," I said, getting angrier by the second. "*You* were the one who ended things and didn't even have the *balls* to do it to my face. And on top of all of that, you went behind my back and scooped up my clients for yourself when Mason and Dunn fired me."

The daunted look on his face confirmed it, not that I needed it. I'd gotten that little piece of information about his worthless ass from Heather.

"Not that I should have been surprised you'd take them. You probably figured I wouldn't mind since I got most of your damn clients for you anyway."

Piece of shit.

I stood to leave. Lee reached out and latched his hand around my wrist.

I looked down at his hand and then at him, my eyes narrowing to thin slits.

"You've got half a second to get your filthy hand off me before I break your fucking finger."

He snatched his hand away. He knew not only that I *could* do it, but that I would without blinking.

"Is everything all right, Miss?"

The waiter had returned with my drink.

"Everything is fine," I said, as he placed the drink on the table.

I pulled out a large bill and handed it to him.

"Keep the change, sweetie," I said, gathering my things.

"Car–"

"We have nothing left to say to each other, Lee. And if you see me at another event, stay the hell away from me."

I turned to leave, but then had one last thought.

"By the way," I said, looking at him. "My...*friend* isn't a downgrade from you. He's an upgrade. In *every* way possible."

My eyes drifted downward slightly, causing Lee to look down as well.

I swung around and my purse knocked over my fresh drink...right into Lee's lap.

He swore, and I smiled as I headed for the elevator and up to my room.

CHAPTER SEVENTEEN

Carmen

"D addy, where's Mindy?"

My father, Eldridge Jones, looked up at me.

We were sitting on the back porch of his house having lunch. The salty sea air filled my nostrils, lulling me into a sense of serenity.

I really needed to get out here more often. It was so peaceful.

My father cleared his throat as he set his utensils down. "Mindy's gone, honey."

I cut into the steak that he'd barbecued and nodded my head absently.

"Did she go shopping or something?" I asked, before biting the steak.

Mindy, my stepmother, had always loved to shop. I just knew that moving out to L.A. where some of the best shopping in the world could be done, had been music to her ears.

"No, Car," he said, quietly. "She's...gone."

I looked at my father, *really* looked at him. That's when I saw the emotions in his eyes. Hurt, betrayal, sadness.

"What happened?" I gasped, dropping my knife and fork.

"We...we grew apart, Car," he said. "It just wasn't working."

I sat there stunned. While Mindy could be superficial, she'd loved my father, and me.

"I...I can't believe this."

"She didn't love me the way I loved her anymore," he said. "I stuck around in a marriage that didn't work once and look what happened. I wasn't about to do it twice."

I nodded my head in sad understanding. My mother had loved her pills more than she loved us, or at least that's how it always felt. Her addiction took her life and left us heartbroken, until Mindy came along.

And now she was gone too.

"How long ago did this happen?" I asked.

"'Bout six months."

"*Six months?*" I screeched. "Why didn't you tell me, Daddy?"

My father picked up his knife and fork and went back to cutting his food.

"Why didn't you tell me about losing your job?"

My eyes grew wide at my father's question. He looked up at me and nodded.

"How did you find out?"

"Donatello."

Damn Donnie.

My father and Donnie had met on one of his trips to visit me. They'd hit it off right away and had become good friends. Apparently, they kept in touch more than even I realized.

"So, young lady," my father started. He was demanding that I explain myself.

I told him the entire story. Including Lee's under-handed part in jacking my clients. That part *really* pissed him off. He'd liked Lee, was confused when I told him that we'd broken up.

"But things are good now?" he asked when I was finished.

"Yes, Daddy," I assured him. "Business is beginning to boom."

"I'm not happy that you kept all of this from me," he said. "But I'm glad everything is working out for you."

"Me too," I said. "Now, back to Mindy."

My father shook his head, but I gently pressed. "Why didn't you tell me?" I asked again.

Dad sighed. "There just never seemed like an ideal time to bring it up."

I definitely understood that, so I decided not to push anymore. He didn't want to talk about it and I respected his wishes. While he did seem to still be out of sorts over it, he also seemed to be coping well. I thought about what he said about not wanting to stay in a marriage that wasn't working, even if it was the second time.

I felt awful for my father, he deserved to be happy. He'd done such a great job loving and raising me.

I wished that he'd be able to find a love that was truly unconditional.

Sebastian

"See you tomorrow, boss."

I walked Suzette out and then locked the door to the store and pulled all the shades down. It was the middle of the week and 154 wasn't open tonight. I always picked this night to stay late to check my inventory. I stuck my earbuds in my ears and got to work. Thirty minutes in, I heard a faint knocking. I pulled the earbuds out and the knocking grew distinctly louder.

I smiled as I headed for the door, wondering what Suzette had forgotten – a regular occurrence.

My smile faded to shock when I saw who was standing outside. My pace quickened as I went to the door, unlocked it and let her in.

"I thought your flight wasn't until tomorrow?" I asked.

"I caught an earlier one," Carmen said, dropping her bag and throwing her arms around my neck. I caught her by the waist and pulled her even closer to me, as our tongues danced in a kiss that revealed just how much we'd missed each other.

I reached behind her and locked the door.

My hands were in her hair, tangled in her curls as her fingers danced along the waves on my head. That shit drove me wild.

Her hands moved from my head, down my chest and then she slid her hand beneath my T-shirt, and her fingers grazed my stomach, causing it to clench. My grip on her hair tighten slightly when she rocked against my erection.

I broke the kiss off and took her hand, pulling her down the front aisle of the store. I pushed her against a wall between two bookshelves, where I started kissing her again, this time reaching down to grab her ass and push her against me even harder.

She'd looked amazing standing at the door in that black and white striped high-waisted pencil skirt that stopped at her knees and a yellow long-sleeved crop top that showed just a hint of skin. Wanting to see – *needing* to feel – more of her skin, I lifted her top up revealing her black bra.

Her head fell back against the wall when I dipped my head to lick the tops of her breast.

"Bas..." she moaned.

"Dammit, I missed you, Bun," I whispered.

"Show me."

I shoved her skirt up and groaned when I discovered that she wasn't wearing any panties underneath her tight skirt.

She went to work undoing my pants, as I pulled my wallet out to grab a condom. She yanked my pants down while I sheathed myself, and then hauled her up into my arms. She kissed me as she wrapped her legs around my waist and I sank into her silky folds.

I reached up and pulled the cups of her bra down with one hand, and wrapped my mouth around one of her tits. I pulled her nipple between my teeth biting just hard enough for her to feel a small amount of pain, but a large amount of pleasure. I knew I'd done it right, but the way she bucked against me, bouncing up and down on my dick.

I squeezed her breast as I kept sucking and biting it. I moved to the other, worshiping it the same way, teasing her with that same pain and pleasure I'd given the first one.

Her thighs tightened around my waist, her walls clamped around my dick and I knew she was about to come.

I was right there with her.

"Shit, Carmen," I grunted.

There was something oddly arousing hearing her sexy

little mewls fill my bookstore. We lost our rhythm and I furiously pounded her pussy over and over and she matched my insane thrusts.

"Sebastian," she screamed, and I let out my own growl that sounded extremely primal.

We stood there for several moments, one of my arms braced against the wall, so I wouldn't put all my weight on her, while she stayed clutched to my body.

I could feel her body trembling with aftershocks of her orgasm. Every time she shifted even slightly, she milked my dick a little and it made me want to fuck her all over again.

I finally pulled out of her and took a step back, after she unhooked her legs from around me and planted her feet back on the ground.

"You sure know how to welcome a girl back home, Kincaid," Carmen said, as she tugged down her skirt, her eyes filled with a wicked gleam.

I shook my head and pulled the condom off, making sure to tie it up. I pulled my pants up and kissed her again.

"Be right back," I said, and headed for the bathroom.

After I got cleaned up, I came back out and found her waiting for me at the bar.

"How was your trip?" I asked, sitting down next to her.

"Productive," she said.

"And your visit to see your dad?"

Her smile dipped slightly at that. "Enlightening."

"How so?"

"Well," She shifted in her seat. "I found out that he already knew that I'd been fired, so I finally told him exactly what happened. And he told me that his marriage is over."

"What?" I asked shocked.

Carmen had mentioned her stepmother before. She'd

never had anything bad to say about her, but I could tell that she now had a bit of animosity toward the woman who'd broken her father's heart. I guess that was to be expected.

"I'm sorry about your dad, Bun," I said, rubbing the back of her neck.

"He was excited for me about my journey in self-employment, though," she said proudly.

Consider yourself lucky, I thought to myself.

"You okay?"

I looked up and noticed her eyes filled with concerned.

"Of course," I said, trying to figure out what I'd done for her to pick up the shift in my mood.

She wasn't buying my answer. Her eyes narrowed and she studied me, trying to figure me out.

Finally, I sighed and said, "I was just thinking that you're lucky that your father 'approves' of your choice to do your own thing."

"Yours doesn't."

It wasn't a question. It was a deduction.

I shook my head, growing uncomfortable.

"Let's just say, he more or less disowned me when I decided that teaching wasn't my thing."

Carmen looked shocked and confused.

"But you're still spreading the joy of literacy. Just in your own way. He has to see this and get that."

"Maybe, if he ever actually came to see it, he'd understand that, but..." I shrugged and then stood and went behind the bar.

I needed a drink.

"I'm sorry, Bas," Carmen said, quietly.

"It is what it is," I said, taking a shot, letting the burn take over my thoughts.

After a moment of silence, Carmen stood and said, "Why don't we get out of here? I'm starving."

I put the liquor away and nodded.

"That sounds like a great idea. Let's go find some food."

The inventory could wait another day.

My Bun was home.

CHAPTER EIGHTEEN

I looked around the sterile looking room and then leaned over and whispered in Heather's ear.

"You know, most people our age spend their birthdays having a nice dinner, or even going to the club."

Heather sucked her teeth, rolled her eyes and flipped the page of the catalogue she was looking through.

"If you still have a problem with this–"

"I've *never* had a problem with this." I lowered my voice when a man came out of a room and walked past us. He looked at us, grinned and I averted my eyes, leaning in to Heather. "I just want to make sure that you're–"

"Carmen, we've had this conversation. I'm sure. I want a baby and I'm done waiting. Oh! This one sounds *very* good," she crooned, as she read one of the donor's descriptions.

It had been a few months since Heather had dropped the bomb that she wanted another baby. And now, as we sat in the waiting room of a sperm bank on her birthday, of all days, I knew she really wanted to go through with this. Heather was nothing, if not determined, and thorough.

She'd vetted this place from top to bottom, before making an appointment.

"Miss Braggs?"

We looked up to find a smiling doctor waiting for us. Heather stood and I followed her into the office.

The doctor introduced herself as Dr. Olvera and Heather dove right in asking questions. I kept quiet the entire time, until the doctor looked from Heather to me.

"We are so glad that the two of you chose us to help bring a baby into the world."

My mouth fell open and Heather burst out laughing.

I adamantly shook my head as Heather, over a fit of giggles, waved her hand and said, "Doctor Olvera, this isn't my...partner. Carmen is my good and supportive friend."

Dr. Olvera's hands flew to her heated cheeks. "Oh! I'm so sorry. It was presumptuous of me to think that. "

"It's fine," Heather insisted. "I'm sure you're used to it in your business."

"Again, I'm sorry for the assumption."

We finished up the meeting and left. As I started my car, I looked over to Heather and she started laughing all over again. I finally gave in and joined her.

"Did you see her face?" Heather cackled.

I wiped the tears away from my face and turned to look at Heather.

"So, you're doin' this, huh?"

Heather nodded. "Yeah, I'm doin' this. I'm gonna have a baby."

I put my car in reverse.

"Come on, let's go get you a birthday drink. It'll probably be the last drink you can have for a while."

I stared over the cards in my hands, my eyes narrowing intimidatingly.

He wasn't fazed one bit.

"Uno...aaaand out!" Tevin shouted, before doing a little victory wiggle in his seat.

I shook my head as I threw my cards down onto the table.

"I just can't beat you, kid."

"That's 'cause I'm the king of Uno!" he shouted, arrogantly.

The kid was so full of himself sometimes. I assumed it was a trait inherited from his father.

"Come on and let's get this mess cleaned up," I said. "Your mom should be here soon."

Heather was at another doctor's appointment and I was on babysitting duty.

"Hey, Aunt Carmen?"

"Yeah, bud?"

"Did you know that I'm gonna have a baby brother or sister soon?"

I froze and looked at him as he went on collecting the cards strewn over the coffee table. I didn't know that Heather had already been talking to him about the situation. I mean, I knew she'd have to at some point, but...

"Oh yeah?" I said, trying to play it cool. "How do you feel about that?"

"I can't wait," he said, excitedly. I let out a relieved breath. "I'm gonna be the best big brother ever," he added, scratching his neck.

I pulled him into my arms.

"You know what?" I said, palming the top of his head. "You *will* be the best big brother ever."

We finished cleaning up and I'd just sat down to have

lunch with Tevin when my doorbell rang. Heather had the code so she could come right in without me having to buzz her up.

Sebastian had the code as well.

Things had been going great between us for the last few months. We spent as much time together as we could when he wasn't busy with the bookstore and the club or when I wasn't busy with work, which included a bit more traveling to procure more clients. I was enjoying every opportunity to spend time with him.

I went over to the door and opened it to find Heather on the other side, looking miserable.

"Why is it so hot?" she grumbled as she stomped into my apartment.

She'd been taking hormone injections to prepare her body for the insemination process. One of the side effects was hot flashes. Another was mood swings.

"How'd it go?" I asked.

"Everything is looking good," Heather replied.

"You look exhausted, honey," I said, giving her a sympathetic pat on the back.

"I am," she said.

"Why don't you take a nap before you head off?" I suggested.

"I couldn't," Heather said.

"Sure you could. Go lay down in the spare room."

"But Tev—"

"Will be fine," I said. "Right, bud?"

Tevin looked over his shoulder at us and shot a thumbs up in the air, before scratching his neck again.

"Hey," I said in a low tone as I walked with Heather to the guest room. "He's been scratching his neck all day. Does he have some kind of allergy?"

Heather shook her head. "Not that I know of. I'll take him to the doctor soon and see what's up."

A little over a week later, Heather called me frantic.

"*Chicken pox!*" she cried. "He's got chicken pox."

"Oh no!" I said. "How is the poor thing?"

"As good as he can be," she sighed. "I just wanted to call and let you know."

"Well I hope he gets better."

"Me too. Thankfully I had them when I was a kid, so I don't have anything to worry about." She paused for a moment and then asked, "You've had them already right, Carmen?"

It seemed like the moment she asked me that, my entire body started to itch.

"Carmen?" Heather asked, worry in her voice.

"No," I admitted, as I reached up to scratch my neck.

"Go to the doctor. Right now."

Sebastian

I pounded on the door again, trying to keep the humor out of my voice.

"Bun, baby, open the damn door."

"Go away, Bas!" she growled.

She'd called, in tears, telling me that she'd gotten the chicken pox from Heather's son, Tevin. When I offered to come over, she refused.

"I've already had them," I'd told her. But her insistence of me staying away was more for vanity reasons.

"I don't want you to see me like this," she'd whined. "I look awful."

That didn't deter me from staying away.

Whether my woman knew it or not, she needed me. She was just too damn stubborn, trying to be tough ass, 'Cut-Throat Carmen' trying to take care of herself. But it was hard as hell to be cut throat when your body was covered in a rash that itched like nobody's business.

"Sebastian!"

I turned to find Donatello at his door and smiled. Over the last few months of dating Carmen, I'd gotten to know Donatello a lot more. We'd had dinner at his condo several times and we'd even gone to see his opera again. I behaved myself the second time we went – at the opera anyway.

"Hey, Donnie," I said.

"Is everything all right?" he asked.

"Our girl's got the chicken pox," I said. "And she refuses to open the door and let me in."

Donatello chuckled as he headed toward me.

"Well then lucky for you, I have a key," he said, sifting through his key ring. "She gave me one so I can water her plants whenever she goes out of town on business."

Donatello unlocked the door to Carmen's apartment and I thanked him, patting him on the shoulder before grabbing the shopping bags I'd brought with me and went in.

"Carmen!" I bellowed, once I closed the door.

She was on the couch, wincing as she scratched her arms.

"You know you're not supposed to be doing that," I chastised, walking over to her.

"And *you're* not supposed to be here," she said, giving

me some major side eye. "I'm taking my damn key back from Donnie."

"No you're not," I replied with a grin. I placed the bags down near the couch and sat down on the coffee table, facing Carmen.

"Shit, Bun," I said, brushing the back of my hand against her forehead. "You're burning up, baby."

I stood and grabbed one of the bags I'd brought with me and headed for her bathroom.

I filled the tub with tepid water and a packet of oatmeal bath treatment I'd bought. Once the tub was full, I went back into the living room and scooped Carmen from the couch.

"Come on, Bun," I said, carrying her to the bathroom. I placed her down on her feet and stripped her out of her clothes before picking her up again and easing her into the tub.

She let out a sigh of relief and laid her head back against the bath pillow. I could tell the oatmeal was soothing against her skin already.

"Better?" I asked.

"So much better," she moaned. She opened her eyes and tilted her head to look my way. "Thank you."

"Even though you didn't want me to come in," I teased.

"And see me like *this*. I'm hideous, Bas."

"You're beautiful, Bun. Scabs and all."

She splashed some of the water at me and I jumped out of the way, laughing.

"You know, you could still leave."

I shook my head, squatting down beside her and brushing her hair off her forehead. "Nah, I'm not going anywhere."

"What about the bookstore?"

"Rye's got it," I said, shrugging. "Getting you better is my main concern right now."

She smiled and sank further into the water, letting out another sigh.

Half an hour later, I helped her out of the tub, and lathered her body with an oatmeal paste I'd made. I got the recipe from Charlotte, who'd gone through the whole chicken pox ordeal with both of my nieces.

"I have to take the medicine my doctor prescribed me," Carmen said, as she got into the bed.

"I've got it," I said, grabbing it, along with a bottle of water off the nightstand. I handed her the pills and the water and she quickly took them. When she was done, she lied back down, her eyes filled with fatigue.

"Get some rest, Bun," I said, and she nodded. In no time, she'd drifted off and I went into the living room.

I turned on the TV, aimlessly clicking through the channels. Who would have ever thought that I'd be taking care of a woman like this, I thought to myself with a shake of my head.

My phone rang and I picked it up off the coffee table and answered it.

"How's she doing?" my sister asked.

"She still has a fever, but she says her skin is feeling better now that she's taken an oatmeal bath and has that paste on. Thanks again for the recipe."

"Not a problem, little bro," she said. "I can't talk long. I'm taking Aria to soccer practice."

"Kiss my niece for me," I said, and then hung up.

I went back to channel surfing and eventually dozed off on the couch. By the time I woke up, it was dark out.

I stretched and then got up and went to check on Carmen. Her fever hadn't gone down much and that worried me slightly. Contracting chicken pox as an adult was sometimes more severe than when kids got it. But I prayed that wasn't the case for Carmen.

I ran her another oatmeal bath and woke her up to carry her to the tub. I also gave her some ibuprofen for the fever. I hated seeing her sick.

Thankfully, her fever broke a few days later. I had to stay on her ass about scratching, but the oatmeal baths and paste helped relieve that quite a bit.

"Are you sure you're going to be okay?" I asked, as she walked me to the door. I'd run out of fresh clothes and since she was on the mend, she insisted that I go home, as well as swing by the bookstore and see how things were going.

"I'll be fine, Bas," she said. "I'm feeling so much better thanks to you."

I nodded and she rose on her toes to kiss me, then hesitated. I wiped away her apprehension when I pulled her into my arms and pressed my lips to hers. I hadn't kissed her in like a week. It had nearly driven me insane.

She sighed against my mouth and I pulled away slowly.

"I'll be back later this evening to check on you," I promised, as I opened the door and she nodded, giving me a pretty little smile before I took off.

CHAPTER NINETEEN

I rushed into 154 late one evening and found Sebastian working behind the bar, mixing drinks.

He'd just finished pouring a drink and was passing it off to the customer when I sat down on a barstool.

"Hey there, gorgeous," he said, grinning at me.

I so wanted to lean over the bar and kiss him, but clearly they were swamped tonight.

I didn't want to share my good news over the phone though, so I'd come straight over to the club after my meeting.

"Bobby got the movie deal for his books," I shouted over the loud crowd.

"For real?" he said. "That's great, baby. Congrats."

"Thank you," I said, full of giddiness.

"This deserves a special drink," he said, gathering items around him.

I watched him as he expertly put together a drink and then slid it in front of me.

"What is it?" I asked, looking down at it.

"A cucumber margarita with a spicy cayenne rim. I call it the 'Carmen Jones'."

"You named a drink after me?" I asked, picking up the drink and taking a sip.

Sebastian nodded as he wiped down the bar. He slung the towel back over his shoulder and said, "It's full of spice, yet at the same time extremely refreshing. Like someone I know."

He was right. The spice around the rim that would have otherwise been a shock to the system, was quickly doused by the coolness from the cucumber.

Typically, I didn't prefer savory style cocktails; the light and fruity ones were more my speed, but this one was pretty good.

I took another sip, nodding my head in approval and he winked at me before telling me he'd be right back after he checked on a customer at the other end of the bar.

I turned in my chair and watched the band on the stage. It felt good to be out again. That bout with the chicken pox had taken me out for longer than I'd expected. But thanks to Sebastian taking care of me, I rebounded quickly.

My eyes landed on him and I watched as he served up drinks, while making small talk with the patrons. He wasn't in his usual attire of a tailored suit for when he was working at the club. I suppose it was because he knew he'd be manning the bar tonight.

That was one of the things I admired about Sebastian. Even though he was the owner, he didn't just sit around barking orders. Whether it was upstairs in the bookstore, or down in the club, he helped out where it was needed, right alongside his employees.

He made his way toward me and offered me another drink, which I declined.

"How are the plans coming along for Bobby's book launch party?" he asked.

The party was a little over a month away.

"They're good," I said. "And of course, we'll have more to celebrate with this movie deal. They're fast-tracking it and bringing him in to work with the screenwriters to make sure the script for the movie is just right."

"I'm betting he's happy about that."

"He is," I said. "Have you seen the baby?"

Bobby and his wife, Ellie's daughter was born a few weeks ago, but I'd only recently gotten a chance to see her since I'd been traveling.

Sebastian nodded. "I went by the hospital right after she was born and took a gift."

"She's so precious," I swooned.

"Yeah," Sebastian agreed, as he turned to grab a glass.

I watched the muscles in his broad back beneath the black T-shirt he was wearing flex and contract with every move he made. My mind drifted and I found myself daydreaming about what a mini version of Sebastian would look like. Would he have his same smooth, light skin and that irresistible smile? I just knew he'd have a love for reading just like his dad...

I blinked and realized Sebastian had turned and was staring at me curiously, much like the way he'd done the first day we met.

"You okay, Bun?"

"Huh? Oh, yeah. Hey, I think I'd like that second drink after all."

"You got it, gorgeous," he said, and went to work making my drink.

I took a long swing of the drink he placed in front of me, trying to calm my nerves. The image of Sebastian having a child wasn't what had shaken me to my core. It was the image of the child's mother being...me!

I'd never imagined myself as a mother before. It wasn't that I didn't like kids. My life just wasn't really suited for one, in my opinion. 'Cut-Throat Carmen' didn't have time for babies and things of that sort.

But suddenly, this man had come into my life and now here I was with visions of children and a house in a cul-de-sac playing in my mind.

A cul-de-sac?!

What was even more mind-boggling was once the initial shock of these thoughts wore off, I didn't find myself filled with terror, but a warm and hopeful feeling washed over me.

"Hey," Sebastian said, pulling me out of my reverie. "We're closing in about an hour. Can you stick around?"

"Sure," I said, smiling.

"And maybe I can follow you back to your place after?"

"I'd expect nothing less."

He gave me that gorgeous smile of his, showing his perfect set of teeth, and got back to work. I pushed those thoughts I'd had moments ago further into the recesses of my mind to mull over some other time.

Sebastian

"So, Charlotte tells me that you're seeing someone?"

I moved my phone away from my mouth so my mother wouldn't hear my annoyed sigh.

Charlotte and her big damn mouth.

Clearing my throat, I said, "Yeah."

"Tell me about this girl," she insisted.

"Her name's Carmen," I started. "She's a literary agent."

"So she's into books like you?"

"Yeah."

We talked about Carmen for a few minutes until that awkward part of our conversations came up as they always did over the last two years.

"How's Dad?" I asked cautiously.

I heard her shifting the phone. "I, uh...that's why I called, sweetheart."

I sat up straighter in my chair.

"Mom?"

"He was feeling out of sorts, so we took him to the doctor."

"Okay..." I said slowly. "And what's going on?"

Her voice dropped to a whisper and my heart sank at the one word my mother spoke.

"Cancer."

"What?" I choked.

She began rapidly talking, her voice still in a hush.

I shook my head, trying to process her words. It was in stage one, and he was going begin chemotherapy over the next several months.

"I'm coming down there," I said finally.

"He..." She blew out a nervous breath. "I wasn't supposed to tell you, Sebastian. He doesn't want you to know. If you come now, suddenly, he'll know that I told you."

"Even with this, he still doesn't want me–"

"I'm so sorry, sweetheart." I could hear the tears in my mother's voice. It tore me up. "You know your father is stubborn. Even though he told me not to say anything, I felt you had the right to know. He is your father."

"Keep me updated," I said.

We hung up after that, and I sat at my desk feeling numb.

I had my face in my hands when I heard a gentle knock on the door.

"Hey," Carmen said, her beautiful face contorted with concern. "Everything okay?"

I shook my head.

She came further into the office and shut the door.

"What's wrong?" she asked, hurrying around the desk to stand in front of me.

I opened and closed my mouth several times, attempting to get the words outs.

"My father has cancer."

"Oh, Sebastian," she gasped, before wrapping her arms around my shoulders, pulling me against her. I wrapped my arms around her waist, burying my face against her stomach. Eventually, I released her and sat back and told her everything my mother had relayed to me.

"When are you going to see him?" she asked, as if it were a foregone conclusion.

Hell, it had been until my mother told me that my father *still* didn't want to see me.

"I'm not."

"What?" she asked, her eyes growing wide. "Bas, you *have* to go."

"He doesn't want me there, Bun!" I said, standing to pace my office. "He didn't even want my mother telling me that he was sick. If he doesn't want me around, why should I disrespect his wishes?"

"Because this is bigger than him being in his feelings about your career change. This is his *life!*"

"You don't think I know that!" I shouted, turning to face her. "Do you know how much this shit kills me? Every fucking day I have to live with the fact that my choice to open this place was such a huge disappointment to my father that he decided to no longer deal with me."

"Then *you* have to be the bigger man in this situation and let him know that you still want him in your life. You have to let him know that even if he's still upset with you, *you* still love him and you're going to be there for him whether he likes it or not."

"It's not that simple, Carmen."

"It is if you make it that simple."

"You wouldn't understand," I bit out, turning to face her. "You've had the perfect relationship with your father. Always been daddy's little girl. You wouldn't know what it's like to have a parent that doesn't want anything to do with you."

"*I* wouldn't know?" Carmen asked, thrusting her fists onto her hips. Her eyes clouded in anger. "The girl whose mother chose drugs over her until the day she OD'd? I wouldn't know?" she shook her head, turned and swung the door open.

I pinched the bridge of my nose, feeling a migraine coming on, but realizing I'd overstepped with my words. I came around my desk and reached for Carmen's wrist.

"Bun, wait—"

"Don't fucking 'Bun' me right now, Sebastian," she snapped, jerking away from me. She spun around and my eyes grew wide when she took two steps and her feet seemed to buckle beneath.

I caught her in my arms and asked, "Are you okay?"

"I'm fine," she huffed, shoving me away. She took a step away from me and let out a gasp of pain.

"Bun, I think you twisted your ankle or something."

"I told you I'm fine–aahhh," she cried out, after trying to take another step. She leaned against the wall to keep from falling.

"You're not fine, Bun," I said, lifting her into my arms.

"Bas, put me down."

She was still pissed, rightfully so. But clearly she'd injured her foot some kind of way.

"I'm taking you to the doctor," I said, heading for the back door of the bookstore that led to where my car was parked. I unlocked it and slid her into the passenger seat before getting in the driver's side and starting it up.

She sat in the seat next to me, arms folded across her chest, face pulled into a scowl.

I'd have to figure out a way to pull my damn foot out of my mouth.

But first I had to make sure *her* foot was okay.

CHAPTER TWENTY

"This is all my fault, Bun," Sebastian sighed.

Silence. I refused to speak.

In actuality, it was all *my* damn fault. For wearing a pair of wedges that I *knew* I had no business wearing. I could practically run a marathon in stilettos any day. But there was this one pair of wedges that whenever I wore them, it was as if the receptors from my brain to my feet were disconnected. Every single time I wore them, it was as if I turned into a novice in heels, stumbling around like a baby deer.

They were the same ones I'd almost fallen in the day Sebastian asked me out on our first date.

They were so damn cute, but I could never bring myself to get rid of them.

Until today.

Those bastards were going to a charity.

But I wasn't about to let Sebastian know any of that because I was still mad as hell at him. What he'd said about me not knowing what it was like to have a parent who wanted nothing to do with you obviously struck a nerve. I knew he'd only said it because he was hurt from his father's rejection, but it drudged up too many painful memories of my own.

There was a knock on the door and my doctor, Dr. Ramone, walked in.

"Miss Jones," he murmured with his nose stuck in my chart. "I usually have to fight tooth and nail to get you in here for an annual checkup. Now, I'm seeing you twice in one month."

I gave him a sheepish smile, which caused Sebastian to roll his eyes. And that caused me to glare at him.

"I see you've recuperated well from the chicken pox," Dr. Ramone said, finally looking up.

I nodded. "It was rough though."

Dr. Ramone and Sebastian stood there staring at each other for a moment and I broke up them sizing up one another.

"Doc, this is my boyfriend, Sebastian Kincaid."

"So, I'm still your boyfriend?" he murmured, with a lightness in his voice.

"Don't push it, Kincaid," I said, still annoyed with him.

Dr. Ramone, smothered his amusement as he and Sebastian shook hands.

"What brings you in today?" he asked, after they released hands.

I held up my hurt ankle.

"Had a little mishap in my shoes," I said.

He shook his head and set the chart down on the counter and took my foot in his hand. "Women and their shoes, right?" He directed the last part at Sebastian, who – wisely – didn't respond.

After examining my ankle, Dr. Ramone looked up and smiled, "You're in luck, miss. It's not broken."

I sighed with relief, but it was short-lived when he said, "It is sprained, however."

I fell back against the examination table and shut my eyes. I felt Sebastian's hand wrap around mine and squeeze it.

"You're going to need to rest, Carmen."

"For how long?" I asked, dreading the answer.

"A minimum of a week."

"A *week*?" I said.

He nodded, as he pulled his prescription pad out of his pocket.

"You should also ice it to help ease the pain and swelling. Though I am going to write you a prescription for some pain meds. Keeping it compressed and elevated will help with the swelling as well. You can pick up an ankle brace from just about any store." He tore the prescription off and handed it to me and then looked at Sebastian. "And make sure she stays out of those crazy heels."

Sebastian nodded and Dr. Ramone turned and left. A few minutes later a nurse came in with a wheelchair.

Before I could protest – not like I *really* could anyway – Sebastian picked me up and gently sat me down in the chair. The nurse pushed me to the front of the doctor's office and waited with me as Sebastian went to get his car.

The nurse helped me into the car and I smiled and thanked her.

"Where are we going?" I asked when I looked around and realized we were headed in the opposite direction of my condo.

"My place."

"Sebastian–"

"Look, Bun," he said, cutting me off. "I know you're pissed at me right now. And I deserve it. What I said was inconsiderate and I'm sorry. But let's not sit here and act like you're going to follow the doctor's orders if left unsupervised."

"I'm not a child, Sebastian," I said, turning to look at him.

"No, you're just hardheaded," he grumbled.

"You know, this could be considered kidnapping."

"Would you prefer I called Heather?"

I *definitely* didn't prefer having Heather hovering over me all motherly-like. I sighed and flopped back against the seat, staring out of the side window.

We stopped by a pharmacy and he picked up my prescription and a brace for my ankle and then we continued to his place.

He pulled into the underground garage and after he parked, I stubbornly undid my seatbelt and opened the door. I swung my body out of the car, placing my uninjured foot onto the ground first. Sebastian reached for me and I swatted his hand out of the way.

"I can manage."

He took a step back, resting his hands on his waist and looked down at me with a raised eyebrow.

The minute my hurt foot hit the ground, my brow broke out into a sweat.

Sebastian shook his head and picked me up.

"That's what I thought," he said, carrying me to the elevator.

We rode in silence, me in his arms with my arms around his neck. I tried like hell not to inhale his scent, but it was hard not to. Especially when he smelled like the vintage books from his store. He always smelled like books and I loved the earthy, leathery smell with a hint of vanillin.

We arrived on his floor and when we were in his apartment, he sat me down on his sofa. I loved his place. It was very similar to mine and felt like home. And it had an *amazing* view of the city, which I could see from my perch on the couch.

The sun was going down and I watched as the city lights began to fill sky.

Sebastian brought me the medicine and a glass of water and I took them as he tended to my foot. He had propped it on the table in front of me and put an ice pack on it.

"I'll put the brace on in a little while," he said, quietly.

I nodded as I took another sip of water.

"What can I do?" he asked, looking down at his hands resting in his lap. "To get off your shit list."

I sighed and looked out of the floor to ceiling window, thinking, before resting my eyes back on him again.

"Go see your father."

Sebastian

I sat facing Carmen, our eyes locked.

I loved the fire in her eyes.

I loved how passionate she was about things she felt strongly about.

I loved every fucking thing about this woman.

And I knew in that moment, because of my newly realized love for her, that I couldn't deny her anything.

"Okay," I said quietly as I nodded.

She opened her mouth as if she was about to argue with me, and then it sank in that I'd agreed to her request.

"Okay?" she repeated. "Just like that?"

I shook my head as I removed the ice pack from her ankle. I took her foot and gingerly slid it into the ankle brace.

In all honesty, I knew that I'd end up going to see my father no matter what. There was no way, despite all the tension that was currently between us, that I could stay away. I told Carmen as much.

"You were right about what you said earlier. This is bigger than either one of us being in our feelings. He's my dad, and despite how angry he still is with me, I need to make sure that he knows that I'm going to be there for him, even if he doesn't want me to be."

Her lip trembled slightly as she nodded, happy with my decision. I slid over to the couch and palmed her face between my hands.

"I'm sorry for being such an asshole earlier. You were just trying to help and you didn't deserve me lashing out like that."

She answered by pressing her lips against mine. I sank my fingers into her hair, tilting her head back to deepen the kiss. My tongue was exploring her mouth when she suddenly yawned.

I chuckled, pressing my forehead to hers.

"Your meds are kicking in, sweetheart."

She shook her head trying to deny it, but then she yawned again, covering her mouth with the back of her hand.

"Come on, Bun," I said. "Let's get you into bed."

I helped her out of her clothes, and put her in one of my shirts, her favorite thing to sleep in. After I stripped down to my boxers, I slid into bed next to her, pulling her body against mine. I got lost in the scent of her, rather than the nervousness that tried to claw at me at the thought of seeing my father for the first time in way too long.

CHAPTER TWENTY-ONE

I shot up in the bed, as throbbing pain shot through my ankle.

"Ssshh," Sebastian said soothingly, rubbing my back. "I'll get your meds."

His voice was still low and enticing, filled with sleep. I fell back against the pillows, watching as he rolled out of bed and left the room to go to the living room.

I hated the way the medicine made me so drowsy. But I hated the pain even more. Thankfully, according to the doctor, it shouldn't last for more than a couple of days. I still had to take it easy for another week. But even after that, he said it could be a month before I was fully healed.

Sebastian returned with the pills and a glass of water.

He handed them to me, and before I took them, I looked at him as he sat on the side of the bed near me, and asked, "When are you going to leave to see your dad?"

"In a couple of days," he said.

I nodded and then took the pills, swallowing them down with the water.

"Come with me."

I nearly choked on the water I was drinking.

"What?"

"I want you to come with me," he said.

I began to shake my head.

"Sebastian, I don't think that's such a good–"

"I can't do this without you, Bun."

"Of course, you can, Bas."

"Well then fine," he said, amending his words, "I don't *want* to do this without you."

I looked down as he took my hand in his.

"You...you're my peace, Bun. I need you with me. This isn't going to be easy. And if he..."

He couldn't finish the words, but I knew what he was trying to say. If his father *still* rejected him, he'd be crushed.

I was still unsure though.

"I've got work–"

"That you can do from anywhere as long as you've got your laptop, cell phone and Wi-Fi."

I pulled my lip between my teeth, already feeling myself about to cave. When he asked what he could do earlier to get me to not be angry with him anymore and I said go see his father, I'd honestly expected another fight. But I was prepared to argue with him. Tomorrow's not promised to anyone, and the thought of Sebastian not trying to repair his relationship with his father tore me up. So I was surprised when he readily agreed and relieved when he said that he would have ended up going to see him regardless. I knew this wasn't going to be an easy task for him.

"Please, Carmen," he begged in a strangled whispered.

I ran my hand across his hair and down the back of his neck and he looked up at me as I nodded.

"I'll go," I agreed.

His shoulders dropped in relief and he smiled at me. He

turned his head, his beard that he'd been growing out for the last couple of months – and I was growing quite fond of it – scraping against my forearm before he kissed my palm.

"We'll swing by your place tomorrow and pack you a bag," he said. "But for now, let's go back to sleep."

It was the middle of the night, and I was glad that the meds were starting to kick in again and the pain in my ankle eased to a dull ache.

Sebastian climbed back into bed, pulling me into his arms.

"What if they don't like me?" I asked as I began to drift off again.

My body trembled with pleasure as Sebastian kissed the back of my neck.

"They'll love you. I've already told my mom about you and she was excited."

"You told your mom about me?" I asked, slightly shocked.

His head, which was now burrowed into the side of my neck nodded, "Technically, Charlotte told her about you. I just filled her in on all the pertinent details. She can't wait to meet you."

"And what about your dad?"

Sebastian let out a self-deprecating laugh. "He'll probably like you more than he likes me right now."

"Don't think like that, Bas," I said on a yawn. "You have to stay positive."

"Yeah," he sighed, his warm breath fanning over my cheek. He squeezed me tighter around my waist as he repeated my words, "Stay positive."

"Carmen, baby, we're only going to be gone for a few days. Do you *really* need all of this?"

I sat on my bed watching as Sebastian looked around at all the clothes that I'd instructed him to pull out of my closet for our trip.

"I mean, you've got a month's worth of shit out here."

"They're different outfits for different occasions," I huffed.

"You just need one bag, Bun," Sebastian argued.

"One bag won't cover my shoes," I complained.

"Speaking of shoes," he said, holding up a pair of stilettos I'd tried to sneak into the bag while he was in the bathroom getting my toiletries. "You know damn well you can't walk in these."

"Sebastian, I'm not wearing this *thing* when I meet your parents for the first time," I spat out, pointing at the brace around my ankle.

"Doesn't seem like you have much of a choice," he said. "Dr. Smooth Operator's orders."

I rolled my eyes at Sebastian's name for Dr. Ramone. Over breakfast the day after my injury, Sebastian had griped about how obvious it was that my doctor had a thing for me. I didn't deny it, because he actually had asked me out once, to which I politely declined. He didn't seem too out of sorts by my rejection, so I hadn't felt the need to change primary care providers. Plus, like Dr. Ramone had said, we typically only saw each other once a year, if that.

Sebastian's not so subtle jealousy was cute and it reminded me of when I'd found myself jealous of a woman I didn't even know, who'd tried to push up on him once at the club. I made sure to reassure him that there was nothing for him to be worried about.

Sebastian Kincaid was the only man who had my heart.

Though he was annoying the shit out of me right now as he vetoed my shoe options.

"No heels," he said firmly, tossing them back into the closet.

"You're a shoe tyrant, you know that?" I pouted.

He grinned and crawled onto the bed and up my body.

"And you're too hardheaded for your own good," he said, kissing my pursed lips.

He moved to get off the bed, but I wrapped my arms around his neck, pinning him against me.

"What are you doing?" he asked. "We've gotta finish getting you packed."

"Later," I purred, sliding my hand in between us and inside his sweatpants to grab his erection.

"Your ankle, baby," he said, trying to pull away again.

"Needs to be elevated, right?" I lifted my legs, hooked them around his waist and I gave him a wicked grin as I said, "Now, they're elevated."

He shook his head, his face filling with a bright smile, that dimple I loved so much winking at me.

"I guess I could use a break," he said, as he kissed me again while pushing up my skirt.

CHAPTER TWENTY-TWO

Sebastian

I didn't know what to expect being trapped in a car with Carmen for over five hours. But it turned out to be a lot of fun considering the unwelcomed reunion I was anticipating.

Carmen kept me entertained on the drive with talk about some of her favorite books. She had me cracking up as she sang and danced in her seat along to the music. Her low-key affinity for trap music amused me to no end.

Eventually she dozed off, just over halfway through the trip. I didn't mind though; it gave me time to think about how to handle seeing my father again.

I hadn't really planned on what I was going to say to my father when I arrived at their house, the home I grew up in. I just knew that it was past time to figure out a way to mend this rift between my dad and me. Since he obviously wasn't willing to make the first step, the ball was in my court.

He may have refused to speak to me over the phone, but he'd have to hear me out if I was standing in his face.

Though I prayed my father would make it through this cancer, and according to my mother, all the signs were positive that he would, I'd never forgive myself if something happened to him before we got the chance to make things right between the two of us.

"Hey."

I looked over to see Carmen stretching that sexy little body of hers in her seat. Her lithe movements stirred something in me and tempted me to pull the car over and devour her body. But I kept my focus on the road.

"How long was I out?" she asked, her voice still heavy with sleep.

I looked at the time on the dashboard. "A little over an hour and a half. We still have about an hour to go before we get there."

Despite the forthcoming circumstances, Carmen was looking forward to the trip. She'd never been to the east coast and she was excited about it. Because of that, I knew she'd love my childhood home.

"We should stop soon," I said. "For gas and something to eat."

"Sounds good," Carmen said. "I've gotta pee."

Fifteen minutes later, we pulled up to a gas station. Carmen ran, well hobbled since she was still wearing an ankle brace, into the store to use the restroom, while I filled up the tank.

We drove across the street to a restaurant for lunch.

"Are you nervous?" she asked quietly, as I picked over my food.

I blew out a breath and looked out the window.

"I guess you could call it that," I finally said.

"It's totally understandable," she said. "How do you think your parents will respond to you showing up unannounced?"

I sat back and tossed my napkin onto my empty plate.

"My mother will be thrilled. Can't call it with my dad."

Carmen sat forward and reached over to cover my hand with hers.

"I know this is hard for you," she said. "But just know that whatever happens, you made the first move. That must count for something, right?"

I nodded, giving her a smile I knew didn't quite reach my eyes.

"Come on," I said, sliding out of the booth. "We don't have that much more of a drive."

"Wow," Carmen exclaimed as we pulled into the driveway of my parents' home that sat right in front of the Atlantic Ocean. She turned and looked at me in awe. "You grew up *here?*"

"Yep," I said, still looking forward.

Carmen's hand on my shoulder caused me to blink and turn to look at her.

"You've got this," she reassured me.

I nodded and opened the door to get out. Carmen met me at the front of the car, and I took her hand in mine as we climbed the steps to the front door.

I blew out a breath before ringing the doorbell.

The door swung open and my mother stood on the other side.

Her eyes grew wide and her mouth fell open.

"Sebastian!" she gasped, her eyes filling with tears.

"I couldn't stay away, Mama," I said, swallowing the lump that had suddenly formed in my throat.

"Of course not," she said, stepping toward me to pull me into her arms. "I'm so glad you didn't listen."

I nodded when she pulled away.

My mother wiped a stray tear away from her face and then turned her focus to Carmen.

"Is this her?" she asked me, though she was still looking directly at Carmen.

"Mom, this is my girlfriend, Carmen Jones. Bun–" That slip earned me a glare. I cleared my throat and said, "Carmen, this is my mother, Patricia."

"It's so nice to meet you, Mrs. Kincaid," Carmen said. My mother waved her hand in front of her before reaching out and pulling Carmen into a warm embrace.

"Please, call me Patty."

"Patty, I can't find my–"

We all looked up to see my father standing in the foyer.

It was a shock to the system. He'd lost a *lot* of weight and his hair was thinner than I'd ever seen it. The urge to hug my father was stronger than I'd ever recalled having.

Unfortunately, he didn't seem quite so eager to see me.

His eyes narrowed in my direction. The fact that with one glare, my father could make me feel reduced to a ten-year-old boy was telling.

"What did you tell him, Patty?" my father asked.

"The truth, Luther!"

"I told you he didn't need to know."

"He has the right, he's your son."

My father turned as if he was going to walk away, but my mother's firm voice stopped him in his tracks.

"Luther Kincaid, don't you *dare* turn your back on your son again."

My dad turned and looked at my mother with a raised eyebrow.

"I have had *enough* of this. We are a family, and I am sick of it being shattered because of your bruised ego. I'm not going to let you keep pushing Sebastian away until he decides he wants nothing to do with us anymore. I won't have it."

She slid her arm through Carmen's and guided her through the foyer to the back door that led to the beach.

"You two are going to talk," she ordered. She looked at my father, narrowing her eyes as she added, "And when we get back you owe our guest an apology for being so rude."

The women stepped out onto the porch and shut the door, leaving me to face my father alone.

Carmen

"Miss Patty, are you okay?"

We'd walked a good distance away from the house in silence. Thankfully, with the brace on, the pain in my ankle was bearable. It had to pale in comparison to what Patricia was going through. When Sebastian's mother had grabbed my arm – much to my surprise – and led me out of the house, she'd been trembling. I understood why. The two most important men in her life had been at odds and she was sick of it. She was ready for them to make amends.

Whether that was possible, I didn't know. But for her peace of mind, I sure hoped it was.

"Oh, what you must think of us," she said, shaking her head.

"Families are complicated," I simply said.

"You can say that again, honey," she sighed.

We finally stopped walking and I looked out at the ocean.

"This is so beautiful," I whispered.

"You really care about my son, don't you?"

I turned to find Patricia studying me.

"What?" I asked.

"You wouldn't be here, knowing what's at stake between those two if you didn't care."

I smiled at Patricia and nodded. "Yes, I do care about Sebastian a lot."

Patricia smiled back and patted my arm that was still interlocked with hers and then we went back to quietly watching the waves crash against the shore.

"Do you think he's still going to refuse to hear Sebastian out?"

"I hope not, dear," Patricia said. "I can't lose my son again."

CHAPTER TWENTY-THREE

Sebastian

"Y ou wasted a trip out here."

I scrubbed my hand down my face and tried to reign in my temper. That's exactly what he wanted, for me to blow up like I'd done the last time.

"We need to talk."

"Got nothin' left to say, boy," my dad said, turning to walk away from me. "I worked my ass off, providing for you, making sure you had a roof over your head, food on the table. I supported your dreams and all for what? For you to throw it all away on some ridiculous–"

"It was *your* dream," I barked.

My father stopped and turned back to look at me.

"Who in the hell do you think you're talking to in that tone?" he ground out.

"It was your dream," I repeated, this time at a more respectable volume. "You were the one who always wanted me to be a teacher."

"Because that's what you wanted," he shouted.

"No," I said, shaking my head. "It's what *you* wanted. 'One day you'll grow up and be a teacher, just like dad.'"

He'd been so livid, complaining about how I was throwing away my career for the bookstore, that I never got the chance to say these words to him before.

I watched my father as my words seemed to take root in his brain. He shook his head as if he still couldn't fathom that what I was saying was true.

"You were always talking about how you wanted to be just like me," he said.

"What kid doesn't want to be like their parent?" I asked. "Especially when they were as great as you were."

My father put his hands on his hips and looked away.

"You were my hero," I said. "And I truly thought that I wanted to be a teacher like you. But once I started, it didn't take long to realize that it wasn't my passion. I understand the sense of betrayal you must have felt when I said I no longer wanted to be a teacher, but you have to understand, I didn't love it the way you did. It would have been unfair to myself to continue on pretending and being miserable."

My dad stood there, still silent.

"Look, Pop," I said, not really knowing what to do at this point. There wasn't much else I could say to get him to understand my point of view of the situation. "I hate the way things have been towards us. I miss you. The main reason I came down here was to see for myself how you were doing. If my being here is causing you more pain, then I'll just go and get Carmen and we will leave."

I began to brush past him to head to the back door when I felt his hand grab my shoulder.

"I never..." He visibly swallowed and tried to speak again. "I never realized that I was projecting my own hopes on you. As parents, we always hope that our kids will grow up to do bigger and better things than we ever did. That's all

I ever wanted. It never occurred to me that I may have been pushing you into something you didn't really want."

I shoved my hands in my pockets. "How could you? When most of my life I thought the same thing as you."

We'd finally arrived at a crossroads. I was the one who asked, "So, what happens now?"

My father looked out the back door and said, "Now, I do exactly what your mother ordered and apologize to your lady friend."

We shared a laugh for the first time in ages and it felt...restorative. Like something that had been broken for so long was finally starting to heal.

When our laugh quieted down, I looked my father in the eyes. Our gazes held for a long time and it seemed like the things we couldn't quite yet say with words were communicated on some other level.

He nodded at me and I did the same, before he pulled me into a tight embrace that truly had me feeling more emotional than I expected.

"Come on," he said gruffly, when he finally pulled away.

He wavered and I caught him by the arm.

"Pop–"

"I'm good," he said. "I get a little dizzy sometimes, but I'm good."

I opened the back door and we headed for the beach. I saw my mother and Carmen walking towards us. Our eyes locked, hers filled with a hopeful expression. I gave her a small wink, and my lip quirked up a little and her face broke out into a bright smile.

They stopped in front of us and my mother looked from me to my father and said, "Well, it appears the two of you haven't torn each other apart."

My father reached his hand out to Carmen, and when she placed hers into his, he smiled at her and said, "Please forgive me for my behavior earlier."

"Apology accepted," Carmen said, grinning at my father.

They fell into a cordial conversation and I followed behind them, arm in arm with my mother, who was absolutely glowing.

I was happy that I'd decide to come home and attempt to work things out with my father.

And I was even happier that Carmen was here with me.

———

I stood in the doorway of the room where my father was getting his chemotherapy treatment in the outpatient clinic at the hospital.

He was with Carmen, both of them enjoying the sugar-free popsicles they were eating, laughing as if he wasn't sitting in a chair hooked up to a machine that was pumping all kinds of chemicals into his body that were making him sicker while healing him at the same time.

Carmen charmed my father instantly. After she accepted his apology for being rude the day before, we went back to the house where we spent the rest of the day and the evening, which included staying for dinner.

My mother wanted us to stay, but I'd already booked a hotel in the event that things didn't go so favorable with my father. Plus, my Bun had a way of getting quite...vocal in ways that I didn't want my mother hearing.

The nurse, who'd gotten my father started with his therapy when we first arrived, came in and checked his vitals.

"I don't think he's ever been this upbeat during a treatment."

I looked down at my mother, who was watching my father and Carmen chat like they'd known each other for years rather than just a day.

"Carmen has a way of bringing out the joy in people," I said.

"She seems like she's quite the spitfire."

"Oh, she's definitely that too," I chuckled.

"She makes you happy," my mother observed.

I nodded, grinning as Carmen stood and took their popsicle sticks to the trash. She went back over to sit with my father and he said something that had her throwing her head back with a laugh that I loved. My father joined Carmen with a loud and boisterous laugh of his own.

"Yeah," I said to my mom. "She makes me really happy."

"I'm so glad to hear that, son," she said. "Do you see a future with her?"

"Mom..." I tried not to sound like I was whining and she laughed lightly.

"What?" she asked. "It's a valid question. You brought her to meet us. That's kind of a big deal. And I see the way you two look at each other when you think no one else is watching."

Carmen chose that moment to look in my direction and smile.

I couldn't help but smile back and my mother poked me in the arm, grinning at me.

"See! There it is."

I shrugged and ran my hand over my head.

"I guess you could say we're pretty serious. It's been nearly...seven months."

I stood there amazed. Had it *really* been that long already since we'd first met? On one hand, it felt like we'd known each other forever from the moment I met her. On the other hand, time seemed to stop sometimes when I was with her. It was quite a phenomenon.

"Well like I said," my mother said, pulling me out of my contemplative state. "I'm just glad that you're happy. Now if only we could get Rye a nice young lady."

That made me laugh hard enough to get the attention of my father, Carmen, and a few other patients and nurses in the room.

"You sound like Charlotte on that subject," I said, shaking my head. "And good luck with that."

CHAPTER TWENTY-FOUR

W e arrived back at the hotel after Sebastian's father's chemo was done for the day. Luther was exhausted, and Patty wanted to get him home so that he could rest.

Sebastian unlocked the door to the suite and opened it so I could go in first. I went straight for the bed and fell back onto it, looking up at the ceiling.

I was curious to how Sebastian felt about the entire situation, seeing his father undergoing chemo. He'd been quiet on the drive back to the hotel and I didn't want to push. I figured if and when he was ready to talk about it, he would.

I heard Sebastian close the door and moments later I gasped when I felt his hand on my leg. I sat up on my elbows and found him kneeling in front of me, pulling off my ballet slippers. His hands came up to the button of my jeans and he unsnapped it and pulled the zipper down. I raised my hips to help him pull my jeans down and felt a shiver shoot up my spine as his hands danced up my calves and then thighs, which I parted willingly.

He kissed my inner thigh, before sitting up higher on his knees to look me in the eyes.

"Thank you," he said quietly.

I sat up and pulled his face between my hands kissing him deeply.

The next few moments were a flurry of clothes being tossed around as we continued undressing each other.

My hands clenched the sheets, when he threw one of my legs over his shoulder as he slid in and out of me. He wrapped one hand around my ankle, peppering hot little kisses against it, while he teased my clit with his other hand.

"Bun," he uttered roughly.

My eyes flew open and my chest constricted at the sight of Sebastian watching me. His gaze was heated yet there was an air of adoration in his eyes that had me going over the edge.

"That's it, Bun," he said, his movements speeding up. "Come for me, Baby. Come with me."

And I did, oh how I did.

My back bowed, my inner walls clenched and I let out a scream that I was sure would have us getting a call from the hotel lobby in a few minutes.

Sebastian seemed much less stressed now, and not just from the sex. Reconciling with his father had clearly lifted a weight off his shoulders. His father's as well, if I had to guess. And I was glad for that, because I had a great time getting to know Luther.

Sebastian was the spitting image of Luther in looks, although after snooping around at the pictures in the Kincaid's home, it was obvious Luther had lost a lot of weight since he'd gotten sick.

I sat up in the bed, watching as he came back from the bathroom.

"So, we'll head home tomorrow after we check out and swing by my parents' place to tell them goodbye," he said, pulling me into his arms when he climbed back into the bed.

"Okay," I said, as I snuggled my back to his front. Our legs intertwined and one of his hands ended up gently palming my breast while the other and ended up in my hair. He began to massage my scalp as he kissed the spot between my neck and shoulder.

This was my favorite way to fall asleep with Sebastian.

"Bas," I said, as I felt my body begin to succumb to sleep.

"Hmm?" He was clearly falling asleep too.

"I'm glad you got your dad back."

He kissed me in that same spot and squeezed his arms around me a little tighter as he said, "Me too, Bun."

Sebastian

I held on to my mother as she squeezed me like she never wanted to let me go. Finally, she pulled away and I smiled at her as she gently patted my cheek before moving on to hug Carmen. I stood in front of my father.

"Make sure you two come back for Thanksgiving," he ordered. "Your mother missed having you here last year."

"Yes sir," I said, nodding.

"And uh, when I'm done with these treatments, your

mother and I will come up your way. So I can see this book-store and club of yours and Reilly's."

"That would be...I'd like that a lot."

My father nodded, and then reached out and pulled me into his arms for a quick hug.

They stayed on the porch waving until we pulled away and drove off.

"I'm gonna miss this place," Carmen sighed.

I looked over to find her staring out of the window as we drove past the beach. I reached over, took her hand in mine and kissed her knuckles.

"We'll come back soon," I promised.

It felt good to know that we would be coming back and I would be welcomed not by just my mother, but by my father as well.

"Dammit, Bun..."

"One more store, Bas!"

I dragged my feet as I followed behind her with a bunch of shopping bags on each arm.

"I don't think all of this is going to fit in the car," I grumbled.

"It's going to fit," she insisted.

On the drive back home, Carmen's eyes had zeroed in on an outlet mall. She'd been asleep when we passed it on the way to see my parents. What was typically a five-hour trip was easily turning into seven, hell maybe even eight.

"It's not like you can even wear these heels right now anyway," I complained.

"Doesn't mean I can't buy them for later," she tossed over her shoulder at me in an annoyed tone.

"By the way, how's that ankle doing anyway?"

"It's fine," she huffed.

"It's fine now," I argued. Women must have gotten some kind of adrenaline boost when it came to shopping. "But it's probably going to be aching later."

"Two more stores," she said.

"Carmen! You *just* said one."

"I know," she said as we entered another store, "But I just saw Scarlette's Closet across the way, we have to go there. That one is just as much for you as it is for me."

She gave me a seductive wink and began sifting through the racks of clothing.

I shook my head and sat down in one of the chairs the store had the good sense to put in; probably specifically for men who were being dragged around by their women.

"I swear, if I didn't love your hardheaded ass..." I mumbled under my breath.

Her fingers paused on a hanger and she whirled around.

"What did you say?" she asked me.

"I said," I growled, raising my voice, "If I didn't love your hardheaded ass...we'd be on the road. At this point, it's gonna be dark by the time we get home."

She walked over to me, leaned right in my face and gave me a kiss that bordered on indecent for public speculation.

"I love you too, Sebastian Kincaid," she breathed against my lips. She reached down, grabbed my hand and pulled me up. "We can skip this store and go straight to Scarlette's Closet."

Suddenly I wasn't so annoyed by our impromptu shopping excursion. Especially when I saw the outfits I'd get to rip off Carmen later on.

CHAPTER TWENTY-FIVE

"To Robert Archer! Whose debut novel is *already* flying off the shelves!"

The crowd lifted their glasses and joined me in the toast for Bobby. I'd just finished giving a speech on how proud I was to be his agent. I meant every word of it. Becoming his agent had changed my life. In more ways than one, I thought as my eyes found Sebastian in the crowd.

The party was in full swing. We'd decided to have a separate book signing upstairs at By the Books, followed by a more intimate party downstairs at 154 to celebrate Bobby's book release.

This was one of my favorite moments as an agent – seeing my clients' hard work being sent out for the world to see.

Bobby was busy chatting so I decided to circle the room, making sure everything was still going well.

Heather rushed toward me and linked my arm with hers, dragging me off to a corner.

"Reilly just asked me out," she whispered loudly.

"Well, it's about time!" I said excitedly.

"No!" she said. "It's the absolute *worst* time for him to be asking."

"Heather–"

"I can't go out with a man when I'm trying to have a baby with another one!" she said, cutting me off.

"I mean, it's not like you *know* the guy who's donating his sp–"

"But you get my point!" she hissed. "And you see why I shouldn't have said yes?"

"Wait, you accepted?"

She nodded, pulling her lip between her teeth. "I wanted to say no. But when I opened my mouth to say it, a yes came out. I don't know what I was thinking. I *wasn't* thinking, obviously," she panicked. She turned and began to head back to him, "I'm gonna cancel."

"Whoa!" I said, stepping in front of her. "Don't do that."

"Car–"

"Just go on one date with him," I suggested. "Reilly is a sweetheart. What's one date going to hurt?"

She blew out a breath and nodded.

"Okay," she said. "One date won't be so bad. But that's it. I can't let myself get distracted by him."

With that small fire put out, I went back to mingling at the party.

Sebastian

I looked around at 154, impressed with the way Carmen and Heather had transformed our club for Bobby's book launch. The tables that were usually scattered throughout the room were now lining the walls for patrons to enjoy the party. Up front near the stage, Carmen had a table set up for the guest of honor and his wife.

I stood back, sipping on a glass of champagne as I watched Carmen work the room filled with guests. She looked delectable in a fuchsia strapless dress that was high in the front, stopping above her knees, and low in the back, just barely sweeping the ground. I couldn't wait to get her away from here. Maybe I could talk her into sneaking up to my office.

My attention heightened when I saw her face morph from that beautiful smile to pure rage. When she began storming across the room, I looked to see where she was headed and was surprised to see her ex.

The last time she'd been in the same room with him, she'd been at a loss for words. It didn't seem like that was going to be the case this time.

I made my way over to them, hoping to diffuse the situation before things got too out of hand.

"This is an invitation only party," she snarled at him, her cheeks were red with anger, while he stood there with a smug grin on his face. "And you damn sure weren't invited."

"You refused to answer my calls or texts," Lee said. "So this was the only way I figured I could see you."

"I told you to stay the hell away from me," she spat out, trying to keep her voice low.

"You heard her," I said, to Lee. "It would be best if you just leave now."

"This is a private matter, my man," Lee said, barely acknowledging me. His eyes were *way* too damn focused on

Carmen's breasts for my liking. "You never responded back confirming if you received the gifts I sent you before and after we got...reacquainted in L.A."

The leer in his eyes, and his suggestive tone set me smooth off.

"Mother fucker–"

"Sebastian!" I heard Carmen's voice behind me after my fist connected with Lee's chin. I lunged for him and jacked his punk ass up by the lapels of his shirt.

"Not here," I heard Reilly say as he and our bodyguard attempted to pull me off the bastard. I shook them both off me and then shoved Lee away from me, who was gasping for air after the way I'd been gripping his shirt.

"Handle that shit, Rye," I said, heading for the exit.

"With pleasure, mate."

I burst through the door and headed for the stairs. I couldn't stay in the club without being tempted to beat Lee to a pulp. Acting out like that wasn't typically my style; I was usually cool and levelheaded through any situation. I'd been trying my best not lose control and make a scene, but with the unspoken implication Lee had made that something had gone down between him and Carmen in L.A., which was *after* we'd started dating...

Nah, I couldn't just let that shit ride, no matter what my usual M.O. was.

"Sebastian! Bas, wait!"

I hit the button to unlock the bookcase door with my fist, and pushed it open.

Carmen was right on my heels, following me into the bookstore.

"Bas–"

"Why didn't you tell me that you'd seen him in L.A.?" I said, turning to face her.

She looked away guiltily and wrung her hands together.

"Because it wasn't necessary."

"You didn't think it was necessary," I laughed hotly. "Just like you didn't think it was necessary to tell me that the son of a bitch was sending my woman gifts!"

"Okay," she said, stepping toward me, pointing a finger at me. "When he first sent me a gift, we weren't even dating yet. The second time he sent me something was just to get a rise out of me after seeing him in L.A., where I told him to leave me alone. And both times he sent me stuff, it went directly in the trash. So no, I didn't feel like that was necessary to tell you about either."

"And what about the two of you getting 'reacquainted' in L.A.?"

"He just said it like that to piss you off," Carmen said. "Sebastian, *nothing* happened between me and Lee out there, at least not the way he's making it out to be."

She grabbed my arm to stop me from pacing. I was sure Reilly and our bodyguard had already tossed Lee out by now, but I still wanted to go find him and bash his face in.

"Sebastian," she said. "You believe me, right? I love *you*. I would never do anything to screw this up."

I took a few calming breaths and looked down at her, saw the desperation in her eyes. I squeezed my eyes shut and nodded.

"Of course, I believe you, Bun," I said. "But next time, just tell me what's going on so I'm not blindsided by this kind of bullshit."

She nodded.

"What happened in L.A.?" I asked.

"I had no idea he was going to be there," she said. "He never used to go to things like that."

"Hmph and now he suddenly decided to pop up at that one?"

"I avoided him the entire time. He caught me off guard the last night of the conference in the hotel bar. I told him off, and when he got things twisted and tried to grab me–"

"He put his goddamned hands on you," I roared and headed for the door.

"Bas," she said, grabbing me by the bicep. "You know he's long gone by now. And besides, I let his ass know that I'd break his fingers, he knew I wasn't bluffing."

That's my girl, I thought. But I was still fucking pissed.

"He was just jealous from the time we ran into him at that restaurant."

I'd picked up a vibe that he was a fuckboy the moment we met. Tonight only proved my suspicions right.

"I let him know that you're better for me...in every way," she said, looking up at me beneath her long eyelashes.

I blew a breath out through my nose, unable to stop the upward tilt of my lip.

"Every way, huh?"

She nodded giving me one of those smiles that let me know exactly what was on her mind.

"Come on," I said, taking her hand in mine as I led her to my office.

CHAPTER TWENTY-SIX

"Jones and Associates Literary Agency."

My lips turned up into a proud smile at Heather's words as we stood and watched the maintenance man of the building where our new office space was now being held added the name of our company to the directory wall.

Heather had been right about eventually needing to expand beyond my home office and add on more employees. My roster of authors had grown to more than what I could handle on my own. A problem I was more than grateful to have.

The maintenance man shut the glass door, wiped it down quickly and then turned and smiled at us before he went about his business.

"Give me your phone so I can take a picture," Heather said. "We have to document this."

I gave her my phone and she ordered me to stand next to the directory. I gave her my brightest smile as I pointed at the name of my company on the board. I pulled Heather into the next picture with me for a selfie

"These are great," I said, scrolling through the pics. I chose one and sent it to my father and then Sebastian.

Sebastian: That's what's up, Bun. So proud of you!

I smiled as I read his text. He'd been a huge help to me when it came to procuring the space on the twentieth floor of a very posh business building by hooking me up with the realtor he'd used to find the spot for By the Books and 154. With Reilly's wise guidance in the financial department, I'd been able to invest and save the money I needed for a down payment on the space and not go broke in the process.

Heather and I headed for the elevator to our floor. When the cab was filled with the chime of a text message alert, we both reached for our phones. Realizing it was Heather's phone, I glanced over and caught a grin on her face as she typed out a response.

"Is that Reeiiilly?" I sang out, bumping her shoulder.

Heather rolled her eyes and kept typing.

"Yes, but it's not what you think."

"If it's not what I think, then what could he possibly be saying to put a smile on your face like that."

"We're just friends, Carmen. He's cool and we hang out every occasionally. But I made it *very* clear that I'm not in the right headspace to be in a relationship. Especially now."

"Why 'especially now'? I asked.

The bell dinged over the elevator and the doors slid open. We walked out as Heather said, "I went to the doctor this morning."

"And?" I asked, stopping in front of our door.

Heather looked at me with an even bigger smile than the one she'd had when she'd gotten that text from Reilly. Her eyes filled with tears and she nodded.

I gasped and pulled her into my arms.

"Why didn't you tell me sooner?" I asked.

"This was *your* day," Heather said. "I didn't want to steal your thunder."

"This is *our* day, sweetie," I said, wiping her tears. "I couldn't have done this without you. And you know I've been just as anxious and eager as you have been about this baby."

Heather had already had a failed attempt at the in vitro process. It had been quite a blow for her, but she hadn't given up, opting to try the process again right away.

"I'm so scared, Carmen. What if something happens again?"

I didn't know how to answer that, but I did my best to stay positive for her sake.

"Let's just focus on one day at a time," I said, and she nodded.

We went into the office, and Heather went to her desk. "The morning is clear," she said. "But we do have an agent coming in this afternoon for an interview."

"That's right," I said. "He seemed promising."

I was heading for my office when the office phone rang. We both looked at each other confused. We hadn't listed the business number yet.

"It has to be a wrong number," I said.

"Maybe they're calling for whoever used to be here before," Heather said, picking up the phone as I continued to my office. "Jones and Associates. Yes, one moment, please. Miss Jones, line one."

My brows furrowed in confusion and I picked up my phone in my office.

"This is Carmen Jones."

"What are you wearing Miss Jones?"

Sebastian's low and sexy voice came through the phone and had my body tingling instantly.

"*Eeeeww*, really you two?"

"Heather!" I laughed. "How 'bout you get off the damn phone?"

After the distinct click, letting me know she was no longer on the line, I sat down in my plush office chair and swiveled in it side to side.

"You know exactly what I'm wearing since I came to work from your place this morning."

He'd cleared space for me in both his closet and his dresser since I spent some much time there these days.

Sebastian chuckled and said, "You're supposed to play along, Bun."

"Well in that case..." I lowered my voice to a sultry volume, as I said, "Not a thing. Except those red bottoms you got me for my birthday."

He groaned in the phone, causing me to laugh.

"I can just imagine you in your office, with those sexy legs kicked up and crossed on your desk."

"You play too much," I giggled.

"How are things going?"

"So far so good. I still can't believe it's real."

"It's real, you worked your ass off. I was calling to see if you had plans for lunch."

"Nope," I said, shaking my head as if he could see me. "Do you want to meet up?"

"Yeah, I'll swing through in a couple of hours." One of the perks of the building we were in was its location. It was a few blocks away from Sebastian's bookstore. I could totally walk there on my lunch break.

"I'll see you soon," I said.

"Hey," he said, before I moved to hang up. "I love you, beautiful."

My smile widened even more as I said, "I love you."

I got lost in reading through resumes, followed by query letters from authors, and lost track of time. I finally looked up when I heard a light knocking at my door.

"Hey gorgeous, you ready for lunch?"

I smiled at Sebastian, who was leaning in my doorway holding a vase of what had easily become my favorite bouquet arrangement of pink roses accented with purple and pink lavender flowers in one hand and a bag of takeout in the other.

I stood, came around my desk and rose on my toes to kiss his lips.

"I assumed we were going out," I said, taking the flowers from his hand and turning to place them on my desk.

"Figured I'd be your deliveryman today," he said, closing the office door.

"Hmmm, my deliveryman huh?" I teased. "What if I don't have enough money to pay?"

Sebastian dropped the bag on the desk, and wrapped his arms around my waist.

"Your mind is always in the gutter, Miss Jones," he murmured, tugging my earlobe between his teeth.

"You're supposed to play along, Bas," I said, throwing his own words back at him from our phone call earlier.

I squealed when he whirled me around, lifted me up and plopped me on my desk. My legs spread instantly and he ran his hands up my skirt, his fingers caressing my thighs before moving further up to the edge of my panties.

"I'm sure we can figure out some other form of compensation," he said, before lowering his lips to mine.

I'd just let out a moan as our tongues began to circle

each other, when the pounding on the door caused Sebastian to take a step back and me to close my legs.

Heather took one look at us and shook her head.

"Yes, Heather," I said, through clenched teeth.

"We have these new-fangled things on doors called *locks*. You should definitely try them, boss lady."

"Definitely will the next time," Sebastian mumbled under his breath. I glanced over at him and he gave me a sly wink.

"What did you need?" I asked Heather.

"You need to go to Publish Now's site," she said eagerly. She looked like she could barely contain her excitement so I grabbed my cell phone off my desk behind me, opened the browser and pulled up their site from my favorites section.

Publish Now Literary Award Nominees Announced

My eyes shot up to Heather's.

"No way!" I said, clicking on the link. "Bobby got nominated?"

"Along with three of our other clients," Heather said. "But that's not all. They added a new award this year."

I'd just stopped scrolling when I saw the award she was talking about, my eyes growing even wider. I let out an ear-piercing scream. Heather joined in with me and Sebastian nearly covered his ears.

"Literary Agent of the Year?" I shouted. "I've been nominated for Literary Agent of the Year!"

I hopped off my desk and Sebastian pulled me into his arms.

"Congrats, baby," he said and gave me a kiss. Once he

released me, Heather wrapped her arms around me and squeezed me so hard, I could barely breathe.

"I'm so proud of you!" she cried. She released me and hurried for the door. "The awards ceremony is in a few weeks. You *have* to go now. I'm going to go online and order our tickets."

Originally, I hadn't planned on attending the event.

Heather closed the door and I placed my hand over my heart, which was beating so fast from all the excitement. I looked up at Sebastian and shook my head, suddenly feeling overwhelmed by emotions.

"Now I wish we had a bottle of champagne," he said with a smile, revealing that dimple.

"If you hadn't suggested that Bobby find an agent," my voice quivered.

Sebastian stepped forward and placed his hands on my hips. "Then you would have figured out some other way to get here," he said, his voice full of conviction. "I mean they don't call you 'Cut-Throat Carmen' for nothing."

He was more than likely right, but it still felt like his encouraging advice to Bobby had been a catalyst that changed my life for the better, in *so* many ways.

"Come on," he said, lightly smacking my butt. "Let's eat before the food gets cold."

"But what about..." My eyes drifted toward the door's lock.

Sebastian shook his head and chuckled, pushing my hair behind my ear.

"My insatiable Bun...As tempting as that is, I can't stay away from the store too long. Suzette's training the new barista we hired."

I nodded in understanding as he moved away and

grabbed the bag of food he'd brought with him. We sat down and started eating.

"So, of course I want you with me at the awards," I said, looking up from my food.

He grinned at me and nodded. "I wouldn't miss it for the world, sweetheart."

I set my fork down, slightly nervous about what I was about to bring up.

"There's a chance that...*he's* going to be there."

Sebastian's hand clenched around the fork he was holding. It had been four months since the incident at Bobby's launch party. I'd seen Lee at a few more events, but whenever he saw me, he made sure to quickly detour and get as far away from me as possible. Between Sebastian's fist to his face and...whatever way Reilly had 'handled' him, I'd had no more problems with Lee. I was grateful for that.

"Shouldn't be a problem," Sebastian finally said after a minute of silence. I could sense his unspoken words of *if he knows what's good for him.*

I simply nodded and we went back to eating.

CHAPTER TWENTY-SEVEN

Sebastian

"And the award for debut author of year goes to...Robert Archer!"

Carmen and I both jumped to our feet, proudly clapping as Bobby sat in his seat stunned. Ellie had to shake him to get him up and out of his chair. I pulled two fingers in my mouth and let out a loud whistle as Bobby headed for the stage.

So far it had been a great night for Jones and Associates Literary Agency. Each of Carmen's clients who were nominated had won an award. There was one award left – Literary Agent of the Year.

Carmen had been playing it cool, acting like she was more excited for her clients to win than herself, but I knew my Bun wanted the win for herself as well. Hell, I wanted it for her too. She more than deserved it.

"Wow," Bobby said, when he got to the podium and took his award. He looked down at it, shook his head and then cleared his throat before speaking again. "A year ago, I was just a struggling writer trying to make it and now...I'm blessed beyond words. I'd like to thank my wife, Ellie, for always supporting and loving me. I'd also like to thank my good friend, Sebastian Kincaid, owner of By the Books Bookstore – check them out – for the endless supply of caffeine, staying open late so I could finish the chapter I was working on when I was in the zone, and the constant words of encouragement."

Bobby's eyes locked with Carmen's and he blew out a breath. "And finally, I'd like to thank the woman who saw something in me and my writing that no one else seemed to see. She rallied for me, fought for me and second to my wife, she has been my biggest supporter. She took a chance on me when we were both down and out." He looked down at the award again and laughed. "We sure showed them, didn't we? Carmen Jones, I couldn't ask for a better agent. This wouldn't have been possible without you."

Carmen smiled and blew a humble kiss his way and the crowd began to applaud again as Bobby left the stage. Carmen stood again and like she'd done with her other clients, she pulled Bobby into a hug. But this one lingered a little longer. It was obvious they were both trying to keep it together. When Carmen sat back down, I passed her a handkerchief and gently rubbed her back.

"You okay?"

She looked at me and nodded, dabbing her eyes.

They went through a few more awards before they finally got to the Literary Agent of the Year category. She reached over and clutched my forearm, her nails digging into my skin even through the layers of my suit jacket and dress shirt. I slid her hand down to mine and interlocked our fingers.

"And the award for Literary Agent of the Year goes to...Carmen Jones, founder of Jones and Associates Literary Agency!"

I vaulted out of my chair, nearly yanking Carmen's arm out of place. Much like Bobby's reaction, Carmen sat there frozen in disbelief.

"Carmen," I said, excitedly, sitting back down. "Bun, baby, you did it."

She turned and looked at me and I covered her mouth with mine. I felt her palm my face and then I broke off the kiss and stood, pulling her up with me and gently propelled her forward toward the stage. I watched as her colleagues and clients in the industry stood, clapping and patting her on the arms as she walked up to the podium.

When she received her award, she stepped up to the microphone, shut her eyes and was quiet for a second, clearly taking in the moment.

"I'm truly at a loss for words right now," she said in a near whisper. "I want to thank my clients for trusting me with their livelihoods, especially Robert Archer. Bobby, *you* were the one who took a chance on *me*. And I'm forever grateful that you were the first client with Jones and Associates. My assistant and dear friend, Heather Braggs, you keep me sane in this business. And last but *definitely* not least, the man that I feel helped put things in motion for me to get to this point of my life, Sebastian Kincaid. You've been supporting me since I first embarked on this journey. I love you so much, baby. Thank you."

When she was done with her speech, she looked over at a table and lifted her award with a bit of a smug grin on her face. It wasn't hard to figure out she was giving a subtle middle finger to the firm who'd fired her.

I stood to my feet again and clapped, a proud smile covering my face.

She came back to the table and I pulled her into my arms for another deep kiss.

The ceremony portion of the evening ended soon after that and a DJ began playing music for the attendants to dance and enjoy the rest of the evening. We shared a few dances and then got out of there and went back to my place.

Once we were in the apartment, I took off my jacket, loosened my tie and went over to the bar to pour a glass of Hennessy. I watched Carmen kick off her shoes as she twirled around with the award in her hand.

"Can you believe it, Bas?" she sighed, her eyes full of delight. She set the award down and stared at it.

I took a sip of my drink and came up behind her, wrapping an arm around her waist. I nodded and then kissed her neck. "Of course I believe it. The things you've done for your clients in nearly a year have been amazing. You deserved to be acknowledged for your accomplishments."

She turned in my arms and reached for my glass, taking a sip. I finished off the drink and set the glass on the table next to her award. Carmen slid her arms around my neck and pulled me down for a kiss. Her tongue – mixed with her own sweet flavor and the cognac – circled mine before I pulled her bottom lip between my teeth. I lifted her into my arms and carried her into the bedroom, kissing her neck and collarbone.

I sat her back down once we got to the room and her hands went to work on the buttons of my shirt while I pulled the pins out of her hair. I toed out of my shoes, and got out of my dress slacks and then went for the zipper on the side of Carmen's dress. It pooled to her feet and then we tumbled in the bed, Carmen on top of me.

She kissed my lips again, and then worked her way down, kissing my neck and my chest. My abs clenched when she ran her tongue across the muscles there, in anticipation for where she was headed.

"Shit, Bun," I rasped when she took me into her hot, wet mouth. I tried to sit up on my elbows and watch her as she sucked my dick, running her tongue up one side around the tip and then back down the other side, her fingers dancing across the veins as she jerked me off at the same time. But the sensations shooting through my body, especially when she looked me right in the eyes and serviced me, had me collapsing back onto the bed, and shutting my eyes.

The scent of her arousal filled the air, and the need to taste her consumed me. I pulled her up, regretfully breaking the connection of her mouth from my dick, and spun her body around so her legs were straddling my head.

I palmed both of her ass cheeks and pulled her sweet pussy to my lips. Carmen let out a moan as she ground against my face. My tongue circled her clit, and then I sucked on it until she began panting harshly.

My hips bucked when I felt her mouth on me again, her hand wrapping around the base. I slid my tongue deeper inside of her, feasting on her juices, as her hand slid up and down my shaft. Her legs began to tremble at the same time as my balls began to tingle.

I broke the connection again, and grabbed a condom off the nightstand.

"Come ride me," I ordered.

She turned around, as I tore the wrapper open and sheathed myself and she took me in, inch by inch. She planted her hands on my chest as she slowly rose and fell over me. It didn't take long for her movements to become erratic and untamed.

"Bas!" she screamed.

"Dammit, I love you, Carmen."

"I love you too," she heaved, before I felt her walls tighten around me, causing me to let out a savage groan. I grabbed her neck, running my thumb along her collarbone before I pulled her down, crushing our lips together as we both came.

Carmen clung to my body as we both fought to catch our breath. Soon her breathing slowed and I looked down to find that she'd fallen asleep, her hair splayed across my chest. I kissed her forehead and gently rolled her off me so I could go and throw away the condom.

When I got back to the room, I stood for a moment, watching her sleep on her side of the bed. It was definitely her side – she belonged there.

I wanted her there. Hell, I *needed* her there every fucking night.

And I was going to make it happen.

I walked into By the Books and smiled when I saw Sebastian. Like the first time I'd ever laid eyes on him, he was behind the bar, in that black shirt, leaning against a pillar with a book in his hands.

I didn't even try to contain the moan that escaped my lips, which earned me a curious glance from an older woman who was leaving the store. She looked over her shoulder at Sebastian and then bumped my arm.

"He is quite delicious, isn't he? I tell ya, if I was about thirty years younger..." she winked and left the store. I turned back and looked at him, thinking about how I didn't have to wonder about 'what if' where Sebastian was concerned.

He was all mine.

I still couldn't believe that it had been a year since I'd first stepped foot into the bookstore. So much had happened in that time. Bobby's book and movie deals and both of us winning awards. In between all of that, we'd celebrated our first holiday season together. We'd gone to visit Patty and Luther – who was now in remission – for Thanksgiving.

They also came to visit us so Luther could finally visit By the Books and 154. He'd been thoroughly impressed and I'll never forget the look of pride on Sebastian's face.

Sebastian finally got to meet my father at Christmas when he came to visit from L.A. With a new girlfriend.

We rang in the New Year, kissing at the stroke of midnight at 154.

It had been the best year for me so far and I had a feeling it was only the beginning for Sebastian and me.

Sebastian looked up from his book and his eyes locked with mine. He smiled, tucked a napkin between the pages to bookmark his place, shut his book and put it away under the bar, before coming from behind the bar to greet me.

"Hey there," he said, pulling me into his arms.

"Hi," I said, before lifting my mouth to accept his kiss.

"I've got a new book for you to check out," he said.

"Really?" I asked. "I'm assuming it's good?"

"Best one I've read in a long time," he said, grinning. "I left it on the table in our spot."

"I'll run up and go get it."

"I'll meet you up there after I lock up."

I headed for the stairs, but slowed down when half way up, I noticed the steps were now covered in pink and purple flower petals. I continued up the stairs and gasped when the lights suddenly went out. I looked up and saw twinkling lights above me, illuminating the bookstore.

I made it to the table, where the trail of petals ended, and found the book Sebastian left there for me.

I opened it and my eyes filled with tears when I discovered the book was hollowed out and there was a velvet box sitting inside. I spun around to find Sebastian standing there, looking at me.

"Sebastian," I whispered before looking down at the book again.

"From the moment I looked up to find you staring at me a year ago," he said, walking towards me, "I knew that there was something special about you."

I couldn't stop the tears as he pulled the box out of the book, and dropped down to one knee.

"Carmen Jones, I want to spend the rest of my life with you." He opened the box, revealing a gorgeous ring as he asked, "Will you marry me?"

I felt lightheaded with joy as I nodded my head.

"Yes," I said. "Yes, I'll marry you."

He smiled as he stood, slid the ring on my finger, and then pulled me in for a deep kiss, in the spot where we'd first began to fall in love...

By the books.

The End

Thanks for reading!

BOOKS BY TÉ

McAllister Friends

Dream Lover

Taking Chances

Always You

McAllister Family Series

After the Storm

Just One Kiss

Perfection

Love After War

Just One Night

Just Once Touch

Reckless Love (A McAllister Family/McAllister Security
Crossover)

The Coalton, Texas Novella Series

Homecoming

Sanctuary

Reawakening

Destined

Irresistible

Four Seasons of Love Series

A Spring Affair

Sultry Summer Nights

Autumn Kisses

A Winter Rendezvous

In The Line of Love Series

Let Me Love You

Love's Taken Over

Book 3 (2017)

The Nobles of Sweet Rapids

Noble Love

Noble Surrender

Noble Redemption

Noble Seduction

McAllister Security

Reckless Love (A McAllister Family/McAllister Security Crossover)

Book 2 (2017)

Love by the Books

KEEP IN TOUCH!

Keep in touch!
Facebook: www.facebook.com/TeRussNovels & www.
facebook.com/TeRussAuthor
Twitter: www.twitter.com/TeRussNovels
Blog: www.terussnovels.blogspot.com
Email: terussnovels@gmail.com

Love by the Books

Published by Shanté Russ

© 2017, Té Russ

Made in United States
Orlando, FL
23 January 2022